W9-CME-761

JFIC
Sherwood:

DEMCO

SHERWOOD

SHERWOOD

ORIGINAL STORIES FROM THE
WORLD OF ROBIN HOOD

Edited by JANE YOLEN
Paintings by DENNIS NOLAN

PHILOMEL BOOKS ◆ NEW YORK

Compilation copyright © 2000 by Jane Yolen
Illustrations copyright © 2000 by Dennis Nolan
All rights reserved. This book, or parts thereof, may not be reproduced
in any form without permission in writing from the publisher,
Philomel Books, a division of Penguin Putnam Books for Young Readers,
345 Hudson Street, New York, NY 10014.
Philomel Books, Reg. U.S. Pat. & Tm. Off. Published simultaneously in Canada.
"Welcome to Sherwood Forest" and
"Our Lady of the Greenwood" © 2000 by Jane Yolen
"Marian" © 2000 by Maxine Trottier
"Under the Bending Yew" © 2000 by Anna Kirwan
"Know Your True Enemy" © 2000 by Nancy Springer
"The Children's War" © 2000 by Timons Esaias
"Straight and True" © 2000 by Robert J. Harris
"At Fountain Abbey" © 2000 by Mary Frances Zambreno
"Robin Hood v. 1.5.3" © 2000 by Adam Stemple
Printed in the United States. Book design by Marikka Tamura
and Gunta Alexander. The text is set in Galliard.

Library of Congress Cataloging-in-Publication Data
Sherwood: original stories from the world of Robin Hood / edited by Jane Yolen;
with paintings by Dennis Nolan. p. cm.
Contents: Welcome to Sherwood Forest / Jane Yolen—Our Lady of the
Greenwood / Jane Yolen—Marian / Maxine Trottier—Under the
bending yew / Anna Kirwan—Know your true enemy / Nancy
Springer—The children's war / Timons Esaias—Straight and true /
Robert J. Harris—At Fountain Abbey / Mary Frances
Zambreno—Robin Hood v. 1.5.3 / Adam Stemple.
1. Robin Hood (Legendary character)—Juvenile fiction.
2. Children's stories, American. [1. Robin Hood (Legendary character)—Fiction.
2. Short stories.] I. Yolen, Jane. II. Nolan, Dennis, ill. PZ5.S5195 2000
[Fic]—dc21 97-47765 CIP AC ISBN 0-399-23182-X
1 3 5 7 9 10 8 6 4 2
First Impression

To Paula Sigman-Lowry,
who has right merrily dwelt within the depths
of Sherwood Forest lo! these many years!
At least in her imagination.—J. Y.

To Abbot Mills.—D. N.

LIST OF ILLUSTRATIONS

Contents

WELCOME TO SHERWOOD FOREST

Give ear and listen, gentlemen,
Who are of freeborn blood,
I shall tell you of a good yeoman
His name was Robin Hood.

—*A Gest of Robyn Hode*
(translated)

Or Robin of the Hood or Robin of the Wood or Robyn Hode or Robin Goodfellow or Robin the Bobbin or Robin of Locksley, the earl's son. Robin Hood has had many names, many faces. He is more legend than man, and the legend began over six hundred years ago. The man—if he really ever existed—lived long before that.

What we know of the medieval Robin comes from five ballads and a bit of a play, the earliest from 1450, though there were even earlier mentions of the tales. What we know of Robin today has been greatly enhanced by years of songs, poems, stories, novels, movies, and television shows. There are even group discussions about the denizens of Sherwood Forest on the Internet, which I have read with great interest.

I first came upon Sherwood's Robin in a wonderful book

called *The Merry Adventures of Robin Hood* by Howard Pyle when I was about eight years old. I don't know which I enjoyed more, the story or the incredible pictures. The characters in Pyle's rollicking book were all heroic, larger than life, and they all spoke what I call *forsoothly:* "Ye said I was no archer, but say so now again!" and "Stand back thine own self, for the better man, I wot, am I."

When I read Pyle's book, I was hooked for all time, I wot.

My friends and I used to play Robin and his merry men under the trees in New York City's Central Park. We didn't do any actual robbing, of course. But we did manage to terrorize a group of small dogs out on walks with their amused masters. We would surround them and say things such as "Hand down thy purse, ye fat merchant!" to an overweight Pekinese or "Let me relieve thee of thy gold, knave," to a nippy toy poodle, all the while waving sticks like swords and bending imaginary bows at our foes. We left the large dogs alone.

The story of Robin Hood as I first learned it from the Pyle book was not one single coherent narrative but a series of adventures: Robin, upon slaying a king's deer, becomes a hunted man in the great forest of Sherwood. Each person whom Robin meets after that—with the exception of the Sheriff of Nottingham—is won over by his heroism and charm, joining the merry band of outlaws in the woods. Among those so inducted into Sherwood green are Will Scarlet, Alan a-Dale, Little John, Midge the miller's son, also known as Much, and the stout Friar Tuck. They prey on rich merchants, fat priors, and other wealthy folk, distributing what they take to the poor. The sheriff plagues them till King Richard the Lionheart returns from the Crusades and—disguised as a friar—bests Robin in a contest with bow and arrow, then magnanimously pardons them all. The book ends with an epilogue reciting the terrible and wonderfully moving story of Robin Hood's death years and years later.

In Pyle's book Robin is a yeoman—that is a man of the lower classes, a jumped-up farmer—who at last is named earl of Huntingdon by the king whom he served so well.

Surprisingly, Maid Marian is not in this book; I did not meet and adore her until much later.

Did it bother me that later on I would read stories that were tremendously different from the ones in this first book? It did not. Or that the names—and the spellings—changed as well? I didn't care. I was always delighted to discover new versions, and I read them with an understanding that story—like gossip—changes in the mouth of the teller. So when I grew up to be a writer, I knew that one day I could possibly make a new Robin Hood story myself. And finally, for this anthology, I got that chance.

And many talk of Robin Hood,
And never shot his bow.

—*Fifteenth-century proverb*

Jane Yolen
Phoenix Farm

In Locksly town, in Nottinghamshire,
  In merry sweet Locksly town,
There bold Robin Hood he was born and was bred,
  Bold Robin of famous renown.

—from *Robin Hood's Birth, Breeding,*
  Valor and Marriage

Our Lady
of the Greenwood

Jane Yolen

"My Lord of Locksley, it is a boy."
"And has his mother named him?"

Lady Margaret lay in the great bed, her stomach humped up like leviathan before her. Her face was in a dancing shadow, for the candles on her bedside tables shuddered with each passing breeze.

She called the midwife to her. "I feel the child moving."

"The child has been moving inside thee lo these many months, dearie," the midwife said. She was never one to stand on ceremony with her patrons, not even so fine a lady as Lady Margaret of Locksley. *What is she but a brood mare?* the midwife thought to herself. *Wed only for the sons she can bear.* She had little patience with the fine folk in the castle, though they were her living. It was the babies who were her chiefest concern.

"This feels quite different," Lady Margaret said. And then she added, "Oh!"

The midwife flipped back the ornately embroidered coverlet and stared at Lady Margaret's legs, nodding. "Oh, indeed. Thy water has broken, dearie. The child will be here before long. Let me call thy women."

"No, Mag, I want only you here," Lady Margaret said. "It will not be a hard birth. He will be born by midnight, christened by noon."

"First children take longer than that, my sweetling," said the midwife.

Lady Margaret sat up and took the midwife's hand, though it was an effort because she was suddenly shaken by a great convulsion. When it was over, she spoke hastily. "Listen, Old Mag, and listen well. This child was promised to the Good Folk ere I came to Locksley's land, that he be a man of the forest, a green man, and their good shepherd."

The midwife sketched a hasty sign of the cross between them. *The Good Folk! The Fey! Whatever was a good Christian woman like Lady Margaret doing mixing with the likes of them?* "What did thee promise them, lady?" she asked, her voice sharp, all pretense of coziness gone. "What did they promise in return?"

"I promised only that they could name the child," Lady Margaret said. "They promised that I might have him," she added.

"And what did thee give up?" asked the midwife Mag, dreading the answer.

"Only my life," said Lady Margaret. She smiled. "Do not look so black, Mag. I have never been hale, girl or woman. Not likely to make old bones, my nurse always said. I have not given up much. And Lord Locksley will have a son. *My* son."

She was shaken by another contraction, much more severe than the first. Squeezing the midwife's hand, she made not a sound till the pain was over. "There," she said, "I feel him creeping from my womb."

"Sliding, more like, dearie," Mag said sweetly, back entire into her old way of speaking. "Just thee work with me and we will have this child born between us as soon as soon."

"By midnight," insisted Lady Margaret, squeezing the midwife's hand again as a third contraction passed through her body, making her belly ripple like an ocean wave. "The Good Folk foresaw it." Mag had never seen the ocean, but she had heard the minstrels sing of it. If it was anything like a woman in labor, she knew she never wanted to be a-sea.

The child—a sturdy boy—was indeed born at midnight. All the candles went out at once from a wind that blew in suddenly through an open window.

Mag held the child, still red with birth blood, overhead. She blessed him silently and consecrated him to the Queen of Heaven, thinking the old words but not saying them aloud:

> *Mary who is o'er us,*
> *Mary who is below us,*
> *Mary who is above us here,*
> *Mary who is above us yonder,*
> *Watch o'er us like a shepherd with sheep*
> *O'er the hills, and valleys,*
> *O'er the steep mountainsides.*

8

"Promise me, Mag," Lady Margaret whispered. "You will take him at once to the greenwood, foot solid and unstraying upon the path. Go all the way to the great oak at the forest's heart. There you will find a circle. Step in boldly. Do not step out again. You will take the care I bid you and no harm will befall you."

"I promise, my lady," said Mag, not at all sure she would do what Locksley's wife had asked. She had never been into the greenwood. It was not a place for Christian folk.

"Or the hounds will be on your trail. That I *can* promise you."

Mag startled. She knew that Lady Margaret did not mean Lord Locksley's hounds, though that would be bad enough. He had brachets and ratters, several deerhound, and a pair of fierce-looking, stiff-legged mastiffs. But Mag was sure Lady Margaret meant the Gabriel hounds, the hunters belonging to the Fey. She knew of them, of course. Everyone did. There was the old verse:

> *The Devil's dandy dogs course*
> *Hell's skyways hunting.*
> *All wise people seek their beds,*
> *The hours of night counting.*

"I promise," she said again, this time meaning it. The fear of the hounds decided her. Though how she was going to get to the Old Forest with the newborn child and find the very place Lady Margaret spoke of, and all in the black of night, she did not know.

• • •

Getting out of the castle with the child was perilously easy. The guards had all turned aside in their watch just as she went past.

Ensorcelled, she thought to herself as she escaped across the moat bridge. Swaddled tight against the midsummer night, the child was still, the dark feathering of his lashes like a bird's wing against the downy cheek. "I will keep thee safe," she whispered to him. "From boggles and nuggles and things that fly in the night." She said it fiercely, but she was sore afraid. For herself as well as the babe.

She slipped down the path that led toward the greenwood. Overhead the moon outlined the Old Forest with a ghostly white light the color of whey. As she went, she kept looking around, right and left, north and south. She did not know what she was looking for, but thought it best to be alert. Once she thought she heard the sound of hounds, but knew it at the last for the soughing of the wind through the trees. All the while the child slept in her arms, that easy, untroubled sleep of the newborn. She hugged him close and moved on.

When she reached the forest edge, where shadows black as raven wings seemed to reach out toward her, she stopped. Hesitated. Changed her mind. Turned to go back home.

This time she heard hounds and it was *not* the wind through trees, for the trees were still.

"Mary who is o'er us," she said aloud to still her galloping heart. Then she turned toward the forest again.

At her voice, the babe opened his eyes. In the moonlight they were not the unfocused milky blue of infant's eyes, but sea green and strangely knowing.

Mag took a step into the shadows, and the dark fully claimed her. She felt herself pulled deep, deeper still into the heart of the woods; the child—his eyes staring up at her—lay heavy in her arms.

She stayed on the path—Lady Margaret had been most specific about that—going past mushrooms that gleamed oddly in the dark; past streams that ran silently, silver against their black banks; past trees that leaned in the night like old men after too many mugs of ale; and over a wide and grassy glade. Little fingers of mist reached out, as if trying to tempt her or pull her off the path, but she kept solidly on.

"Mary who is below us," she whispered.

There was a crying sound, but it was not the child she carried. A white owl, the round circle of its face glowing, flew past her. She felt the wind from its silent wings.

And then—was it a moment? Was it an hour?—she was at the great oak that Lady Margaret had spoken of, its branches spread wide and down, making a kind of woody bower within the glade.

"Oh, my lady," Mag said, then caught her breath. The moon was somehow shining through the green interlacings of the oak branches. And there in the very center of the greenwood, under the spreading oak, the moonlight illuminated a circle drawn in the grass.

Lady Margaret had told her to step boldly into the circle with the child and not to stir from there till night was done. "Not a foot out of it," she had warned. "Not a finger. Else you will be lost."

So Mag, shivering with more than the cold night air, and

feeling every one of her sixty-three years, strode into the circle and, gathering her skirts about her, sat down on the ground within the circle to wait.

She did not have to wait long. Between one blink of the eye and the next, the empty glade was suddenly full of dancing bodies, though one could not rightly call them human. An unseen band piped song after song, and not a one of them was a song she knew.

Among the dancers were creatures scarce a hand's breadth high, the color of fungus. And little mannikins dressed in green with red caps upon their heads. An elf skipped by, holding a lantern made of a campanula out of which streamed a blue-green light. There were fairies no bigger than a singing bird, with darning-needle wings, translucent and veined by moonlight, who flitted about in a complicated reel. But there were larger folk as well, near human size, with long yellow-white hair bound with strips of cloth that glittered like the overhead stars. They were beautiful and terrifying at the same time, and these larger Fey danced in a slow, swaying rhythm that was hypnotic to watch.

And then Mag saw, at the edges of the fairy dancers, ragged human folk, their skirts and trews dirty and torn, their hair tangled in elflocks. They danced, too. And far from seeming sad at their terrible estate, or frightened as Mag was, they kicked up their heels and danced as if they were having a marvelous time. Mag stared at them the longest for they reminded her of something. And when a couple went capering by, holding hands and spinning wildly, Mag gasped aloud, for the man of the pair was Tom the Swineherd, lost these seven years.

But there were larger folk as well.

At the sound of her voice, the Good Folk all turned and stared into the circle. One of them, a tall and fiercely handsome Fey, came over and stood at the very edge of the circle. He held out his hand to Mag.

"Come and join us, Mag, and ye shall be young again and beautiful. I shall be thy consort and ye shall live in my hall."

His words were fair and seemingly open, and for a moment she was sorely tempted. *Who would not be, to be young again. And lovely.* But she looked over at Tom and he was neither young nor comely. Nor were any of the human folk there. And besides, there was something dark and hidden in the fairy prince's eyes. Something she did not like or trust.

"Oh, my Lady of the Greenwood," Mag prayed aloud, meaning the Queen of Heaven, "save me and the child." But meaning and magic are held to different tasks under the oak tree. What she meant was, somehow, not what she said.

Suddenly there was before her, shimmering in the moonlight, the most beautiful woman Mag had ever seen. She was as tall as Lord Locksley and slim as a girl, with snow-white hair tied up in a hundred braids. There were bells hanging at her belt and sewn to the bottom of her green skirt, so whenever she moved she made music. "Thee called me, Old Mag, and I am come."

"I called the Queen of Heaven," Mag whispered, clutching the silent child to her breast.

"I am all the queen there is here," said the woman. "But as thee cried out my name, the Lady of the Greenwood, I must give thee what thee wishes."

"You will let me go?" Mag asked.

"Come outside the circle and then thee will surely be free," the dark-eyed prince of the Fey said. But when the queen turned and glared at him, he shook quite visibly and took two steps back.

Then Mag remembered what Lady Margaret had told her and shook her head. "I dare not," she said. "The circle is my protection."

"Thee will not," agreed the queen. "Till the night is done. But let me see the child's face."

As if a geas, a fate, had been laid upon her, Mag obeyed, lifting the blanket away from the baby's head.

The queen clapped her hands. "That is Lady Margaret's child."

Mag was astonished. "How do you know?"

The queen gave her such a look then that Mag was forced to drop her eyes. The fairy woman might not be the Queen of Heaven, but she was the queen of the *Greenwood*. Of course she would know!

"We have promised to give the child something," the queen said.

"A name," Mag said.

The queen nodded and then, one by one, the trooping fairies came to the circle's edge and gave the boy names.

"Fleet-foot," said one.

"Green kin," said another.

"Straight as an arrow," said a third.

"King's own."

"Child of the wood."

14

"Giver of riches."

"Merry maker."

"Bow bender."

"Staff breaker."

And on and on and on they went. Such odd things, not a good Christian name among them. Mag kept shaking her head as if rejecting every one, till they were all done with their naming.

"A name," the queen said when they were through, "is what one is. It is power and honor and all."

A name, Mag thought, *is but a tag. A man may be born with one name, achieve another. Honor and power come from the heart.* But she did not say that aloud. For just then the first thin red line of dawn shone between the trees.

"Away!" the dark-eyed prince cried. And the rest echoed him, disappearing as suddenly as stars in the morning, one small flicker and they were gone.

Mag waited long into the morning, when sunlight completely lit the little glade, and the Good Folk were gone to their rest. She was just about to stand and step out of the circle, when a little bird flew down out of the tree. It was an undistinguished brown bird with an orange breast. It lit on the outside of the circle, but then hopped in, totally unafraid. Standing still for a moment, it cocked its head to one side and looked at Mag.

"Why, thou art a robin," she said aloud. Suddenly she remembered the story one of the good sisters of Kirklees Abbey had told her: "When Our Lord Jesus was dying, the robin tried to pluck away the thorns on his crown but only managed to tear its own little breast. As its reward, the robin's breast was ever stained to this day in memory of its brave deed."

Why, what better name than this? she thought. *For a child who would be brave and true.* "The Lady of the Greenwood has sent thee thy name, child."

The baby in her arms looked up at her and, though it is said that newborns cannot smile, he smiled.

> *"My Lord of Locksley, it is a boy."*
> *"And has his mother named him?"*
> *"She did, my lord, before she died, poor sweet lady."*
> *"And what name did she give him?"*
> *"Robin, my lord."*

With quiver and bow, sword, buckler, and all,
Thus armed was Marian most bold,
Still wandering about to find Robin out,
Whose person was better than gold.

—from *Robin Hood and Maid Marian*

Marian

Maxine Trottier

When Marian Fitzwalter was six years old, she climbed to the highest point of her father's castle and threw all of her dolls from the wall. Most of her poppets fell into the shallow moat. They floated a few moments, buoyed by their sawdust and the air caught in their tiny shifts. Then they sank into the green, weedy water. The moat pike would nibble at them for weeks. One doll, snatched by a sudden updraft that skittered along the castle wall, dropped into the garden. It swelled up dreadfully. That spring was quite rainy. A nervous servant, new to the household, came upon the doll a few weeks later lying on its back in the roses, all swollen and pale. The woman fainted and had to be carried home.

"You must do something with that girl," said Marian's father.

"The dungeon perhaps?" suggested her mother.

Marian was not a bad child; it was only that she would not be kept inside. Weather meant nothing. Sleet might pelt the castle and drive in every hound, steamy and damp to the hearth. Marian would be out, playing in the courtyard or standing on tiptoe to see what new bird might be in the mews. She did not care for hunting. Still, the silent hawks—hot yellow eyes flaming unseen beneath their tasseled hoods—called to her. Ivy was for climbing; it was much more interesting to scale the walls and fall into a window all covered in leaves and spiderwebs than to enter through the door, eyes cast down, hands neatly folded within one's sleeves. The shallow lake beyond the sheep meadow was for frogging and wading or the picking of tiny spring cattails. And the forest, Sherwood Forest, crouched deep and brooding with a thousand wondrous places secreted within its cool, leafy folds, that was the best place of all.

Finally, wondering what would happen to this strange child, her father threw his hands in the air. Her mother shook her head as she stitched at the endless tapestry she worked each day. Marian's nurse said frantic prayers.

"No one will ever marry her," worried her mother.

"Perhaps she will meet some forest sprite and fall in love with him," sighed her father.

In time, there was a peace of sorts. Marian ceased tearing up her shifts to make rope ladders by which she might climb down the castle walls. They let her wander. In turn, she did something ladylike each day to calm her mother. Sitting amongst the women in a turret room where the tapestry looms stretched, a needle held in her small hard fingers, their tips callused by bowstring, Marian might close her eyes and feel the forest around her. She heard its voice as she slept. A sound of shivering oaks and larches whispered in her dreams. Birdsong and the small pulse of frogs echoed within her heartbeat even as she worked the tiny needle.

Marian went to the forest each day. She would take off her gown and fold it neatly across her bed. She always put on a suit of green that she had carefully sewed herself. Dulled by wear and washing, it was the color of a warm August afternoon, dusty and soft as ash leaves before a summer storm. There was a light tunic of thin wool and hose that matched. She had a longbow perfectly sized to her frame, but rabbits and the king's deer had nothing to fear from her; she shot only at trees. No apple or pear in the kingdom was safe from the arrows of Maid Marian.

Each season she became more a part of the forest. In winter her footprints pocked the snow alongside those of wolves and hares; in summer she grew browned by the buttery English sun. Years later, kneeling in a cloister, praying for the one man she would ever love, she could close her eyes and in her lonely mind smell the crushed ferns and fallen leaves their steps had stirred in Sherwood's shadowed glades.

Marian loved to climb the big twisting trees. She hid there and looked down upon people who hurried along paths running through the forest. Most went about their own business; it was only the sheriff's men who must be avoided. Marian had watched them riding noisily down the path. Their polished helmets and the rattle of their weapons were a cold, silvery menace.

Marian loved to climb the big twisting trees.

Everyone said that Sherwood was full of robbers and outlaws, but Marian had never seen any. Sometimes she pretended that she was an outlaw living in the woods. But without other outlaws it did not hold her interest. How fine it would be to have a friend with whom she might share this.

It would make the forest much more merry, she sometimes thought. Still, she believed there was a bond tying her more firmly to its glades and hidden hollows than any she might feel with another soul. When she went out to the forest on the sunny morning that everything changed, Marian Fitzwalter was ten years old.

It was a fine day for spying. Legions of birds swooped about. Musty droppings spattered the ground. Chirps and coos were a muffled song in the thick of the woods. Then, sitting hidden in a tree above the forest floor, she heard a different sound. It was not the heavy clomp of some friar's mount overburdened by saintly weight, nor was it the dainty patter of a fine lady's mule all jingling with silver trappings. This was the slow uncertain step of a single person. Dead leaves crunched and small twigs snapped. Marian pushed the branches aside and looked down. There, walking slowly down the path, was a boy. Even from her perch she could see his serious face beneath the smudges and scratches. He carried a bow taller than himself.

"Hello the path!" cried Marian in her best outlaw shriek, and the boy whooped in shock and surprise.

"Who calls?" he shouted back. His voice hardly cracked at all.

"It is I, Maid Marian of Sherwood, and this is my forest!" Marian always believed in cutting straight to the chase.

23

"What rot!" called the boy to the treetops. He could see no one. "This is the king's forest."

"No, no, no!" grumbled Marian crossly, dropping from her branch. "I say 'hello the path' and you must say 'hello the trees.' That is the way it is done."

"And what way is that?" asked the boy. He stared at the girl who stood before him. She was tall and as slim as the bow she carelessly slung over her shoulder. Her nose was freckled and her hair tangled. She stood with a careless ease he could not quite equal. A lifetime from now he would look at her across a forest grove and remember this day and the fine slender shadow she had cast against the bracken.

"Why, it is the way of all the outlaws of Sherwood!" said Marian, now quite caught up in her own nonsense, although suddenly it did not seem to be nonsense at all. This boy who faced her looked back with the calm, hot eyes of one of her father's hawks, a kestrel perhaps. She saw herself but could not know it.

"Are you an outlaw?" he asked, and just a hint of mocking laughter was there at the back of the question. Marian's tanned cheeks flushed. She had never shared her dream with another. To think that he might be making a jest of her was a shock as cold and silvery as snow in the mouth.

"No," answered Marian reluctantly. She was not a liar. "I am Marian Fitzwalter. And who are you?"

"I am Robin. Robin of Locksley," he answered seriously. Then in a rather smaller voice he added, "I have wandered these woods a hundred times, but today I admit I am lost." Marian did not laugh. More than once she had tramped through the forest, looking for signs and blazes, anything that might show the way.

"That is not so bad. There is always a way home," she said, and they both smiled.

And so she led him through Sherwood Forest. But first they stopped to watch rabbits nibbling at tender mosses all dappled with sunlight. They waded in the shallows of a brook and tossed pebbles into the water to wake the sleeping trout. In a small meadow, Marian shot her arrows at apples in a tree, seeming not to aim. Soon the grass was littered with fruit, each with an arrow passing neatly through its middle.

"You do that well," said Robin, who seldom hit anything but shot at it all.

"It is not so hard," answered Marian, retrieving her arrows.

They ate the sour apples and wiped their mouths on their sleeves, then walked out from the cover of the trees into a quiet meadow. Shadows stretched across the even, deer-cropped grass. The bees were silent, having long ago buzzed home to their hives, and katydids had wakened and were beginning to call. Gold-red sunlight spangled about in the low branches for a moment and then disappeared. It was evening and night was coming. Lengthening shadows would blur the forest's clear edge. If there was light to see, Marian could find her way anywhere in the forest, but night would turn it into a stranger.

"We must turn back," insisted Robin, taking charge. "I am expected home." In truth, he was not completely certain that he had been missed. The son of a forester, he was always slipping away to roam Sherwood at odd times, and his mother had become accustomed to his absences.

"Follow me," she answered with a hint of a smile.

"Do you know the way out?" asked Robin.

"I know where we are going," she said, and began to walk. Robin followed her back into the woods. Shadows deepened and fireflies danced against a soft mist that had begun to rise. Roots and vines, carefully placed on the forest floor, tripped them. Low branches pulled at their clothing and scratched their faces. They did not speak; the sound of their breathing joined the peeping of tree frogs and the airy hum of mosquitoes. Finally Marian stopped and faced Robin in the darkness.

"Well, we are here," she said triumphantly. They stood in a clearing. Stars glittered above them and one fell, a silver arc across the sky.

"What do you mean?" asked Robin.

"I have found it," said Marian, dropping her bow and quiver. "I know exactly where we are."

"But we are still in the forest . . ." sputtered Robin. "I knew we should have turned back!" *Perhaps we will be here forever,* he thought to himself.

"Of course we are in the forest," said Marian grandly, sweeping her arm around. "We are at the very center of Sherwood, and this is my camp." In the dim starlight Robin could see a small shelter and a circle of stones where a fire might be built.

"Where do you sleep?" asked Robin, dropping his quiver and bow next to Marian's. He had forgotten about going home. The simple camp suddenly seemed quite mysterious and, in a strange way, safe.

"Well, for now on the ground. I have only begun the camp," admitted Marian, "but someday it will have houses in the trees and ropes from which we can swing, and music and food and so many people. . . ." For a moment he saw the clearing with her eyes. Laughter and harps and the good will of loyal companions echoed in his mind.

"Well, if we must spend the night here then we need a fire," announced Robin with certainty. This he could do.

"We will only stay for a few hours," assured Marian. She had never spent a night in the forest with anyone, but she felt no fear. "When the moon rises we will set out." She watched him gather fallen branches and kneel before the ring of stones. Bent over the tinder, his fair hair in his eyes, Robin struck the flint into sparks and blew on the tiny flames that caught.

Marian had never had a friend before. True, he could not shoot and he did not know the forest, but one could learn those things. She had fumbled about herself in the beginning, her arrows hitting anything but the straw target at which she aimed. *He seems right in this place,* she thought.

When flames lit the trees that ringed the glade, Marian went into the shelter. From the box in its dry corner she took a jar with a close-fitting lid.

"I have nuts and dried apricots," offered Marian, sitting down at the fire.

"It will be a feast." Robin laughed. He had not thought to carry food that day. They ate and then drank cold water from the stream that ran nearby. The fire sank. Its embers glowed and trembled in the night's soft breeze.

"How did you find this place?" asked Robin later, poking at the small flames.

"I am not sure," said Marian slowly. She finished a sweet apricot. "One day when I was walking, I ended up here. Sometimes I think it called to me." They cracked nuts and pulled the shells apart for the pale meat inside.

"I would wager that no one else knows about it," said Robin thoughtfully as he chewed.

"Only me," said Marian, leaning back to watch the stars. "And now you." Robin looked up from the fire at Marian's still face. He had never felt completely at ease in this forest. One tree looked much the same as another. Yet he was certain that all of its secrets were waiting there just out of his reach. It should have been hard for him to admit that Marian could do all these things better than he, but somehow it was not. *She will be a good friend,* he thought.

They talked for a while in the firelight, laughing at their ruined clothing and dirty faces. It seemed they were both given to escaping from home. Parents were much the same, they agreed, whether one lived in a castle or in a forester's cottage. The night sighed around them and odd sounds filled the darkness.

"Listen," whispered Marian at the rustling sound of a small animal.

"It is only a badger or a stoat hunting in the dark," answered Robin. "The night is a good time for them to move about."

"We should do the same," said Marian. Robin looked up. A

fine round moon had lifted above the edge of the trees; the clearing was frosted by its light. They threw dirt upon the fire and put away the jar. Slinging their quivers over their shoulders, they picked up their bows and left the glade.

Now the forest was alive with noises. Things moved within its shadows, hiding or hunting, and each cry seemed somehow larger in the dark. A trembling scream echoed above them.

"What was that?" cried Robin, stepping back.

"It is only an owl," said Marian, not unkindly. She remembered the first time she had heard a hunting owl in the forest. Her heart had nearly stopped. Then she learned to call back in its wavering cry. Now she could make the sound seem to come from anywhere.

The wind rose and the old trees swayed, letting moonlight down onto the forest floor. There was enough of a path so that they could walk next to each other. In time, the path grew clearer and finally they could see a dirt-packed road.

"Let us walk along here," said Robin, leading the way. "The going will be easier." He was picking burrs and prickles from his hose and there was a great tear in one knee.

"Wait," said Marian, catching hold of his arm. "I hear something coming."

"No," Robin answered, tossing the words over his shoulder, "it is only the wind."

"The wind does not ride horses," said Marian. Robin stopped. Harness clinked and rattled, a faint chilling sound in the distance. Common people seldom rode through the forest at night. "Quickly!" hissed Marian. "Into the trees."

She led him to a beech with low sweeping branches, and like two young squirrels they skittered into the dark leaves. Below them, the faint jingling grew louder. The steady clop of hoof-beats sounded and a group of soldiers rode into sight.

"It is the sheriff's men," whispered Robin.

"If they find us we are done for," breathed Marian, although she was not certain they would come to harm.

"But we are only walking in the woods," Robin said softly.

"They might think we are poachers. Or outlaws. If we are quiet they will pass by and never know we were here," Marian whispered as the men neared their tree.

"Halt!" called the captain loudly to his men, and the soldiers reined in their horses. "We will camp here for the night and rest." Below them, moonlight glinted dully against polished helmets and swords. A faint sense of menace lifted with the wind, as rank as the scent of sweating horses.

"Are you certain, sir?" asked one of them. "We are not so far from Nottingham."

"After all, this is Sherwood," added another.

"What do you mean?" asked the captain.

"Well, there might be outlaws," ventured the man.

"Nonsense!" laughed the captain, making himself comfortable on a nearby rock. "There are no outlaws. Start a fire. If I say we camp, then we camp!" Robin and Marian stared at each other, their eyes wide. The soldiers dismounted and fell to work. Some gathered wood for a fire; others saw to the horses. Each animal carried many bags tied across its saddle.

"We can't sit here all night," whispered Robin. "They will see us when the sun comes up."

Marian did not answer him. She only winked. Then cupping her hands around her mouth she gave a long eerie cry. It seemed to come from the oaks across the road.

"What is that?" asked a soldier nervously, dropping his arm-load of wood.

"It's only an owl," answered another. A second cry wavered behind them and a third rose from the left.

"There do seem to be a great many owls in the forest tonight," muttered someone. Then Marian made a sound no owl had ever made. The hair stood up on the back of Robin's neck, and the horses below them reared and squealed. There was a scramble to bring the animals and their baggage under control. The captain slapped his thighs and stood.

"Well, then! That's enough of a rest. Mount up!" he shouted, and he heaved himself onto his trembling horse.

"But we've only just stopped, sir," said a soldier.

"If I say we've had enough of a rest, then we've had enough of a rest!" bellowed the captain. "Besides, Nottingham is not so far and the sun will be up in an hour or two." He spurred his horse and galloped off, leaving his men to hurry after him.

In a few moments the dust had settled and the road was empty. Trying to keep silent had been almost painful; Marian and Robin dropped to the ground and lay there limp with laughter.

"What a dreadful sound that was!" gasped Robin when he could speak at last.

"It is ghastly, isn't it," said Marian, wiping her eyes. They struggled to their feet, still laughing.

"Look," said Robin as he bent over and picked up something from the ground. "It must have fallen from one of the horses." He untied the leather thong that held the small heavy bag closed. Inside, the dull glint of gold surprised them.

"Tax money," said Marian. "They were taking tax money to Nottingham. What should we do with it?"

"We can't keep it," answered Robin. "It isn't ours, after all." Whatever the world might say of him, whatever it might think, he would not be called a thief. He and Marian started down the road. They walked along in silence for a while.

"Well, if it isn't ours and we can't keep it, then we must give it away!" offered Marian brightly. "There is a small church near the edge of the forest where this road leads."

"We will leave it there, then," decided Robin. He noticed that he could see Marian more clearly now. The light was tinged with pink and all the night sounds had ended. In the hush of dawn, robins and larks began their morning songs. A cock crowed in the distance.

Finally the road widened, and they saw a low stone building set back in a grove of oaks. Robin and Marian walked, side by side, into the church. It still held the night's coolness and damp. A simple wooden altar stood at the front. Shafts of sunlight reached through the narrow open windows and turned its plain cloth to pale rose. Robin set the bag of gold upon the altar. Later that morning the young friar who kept the church would find it. Many years afterward, when he was plump and bald and jolly and had left his church to live in the heart of Sherwood, he would think back on that particular bag of gold. He had been able to share it with many of the poor. He was often tempted to ask his companions where the gold came from, but in the end he did not. In his heart he knew who had brought it.

Marian and Robin saw no one else on the road that morning. When they were clear of the forest, Marian turned and raced into a meadow. Just over that hill, past the wildflowers and grazing cattle, would be her father's castle. Robin ran by her side. At a shallow part of the moat they stepped across on mossy stones. Frogs scattered and dragonflies lifted from the reeds. Marian showed him the best handholds in the ivy and together they climbed the castle's wall up one side and down the other. The household was just stirring. Hounds wagged their tails sleepily as Marian passed; she hoped only they had seen her slip away yesterday. In the enormous kitchen, Cook was baking. Her dear round face was damp and pink; a smell of new bread hung around her.

"We are outlaws," said Marian. "Do you have any gold?"

"No, but you may each have a piece of bread and honey," said Cook dryly. "And I would waste no time getting up to your lady mother's rooms, my girl. They are none too pleased with you having been out and about again all night."

Marian sighed. She led Robin out to the kitchen garden and they sat leaning against the sun-warmed wall eating their booty. Wasps buzzed heavily in the sunshine, drowsy with juice from fallen pears and apricots. The moment was very sweet, and suddenly they both felt tired.

"It will mean extra hours at the loom, I expect," said Marian, stretching her arms over her head. Robin wondered how many logs he would be ordered to chop into firewood.

"Might we do this again?" asked Robin hopefully as he stifled a yawn. "It was so much fun. I do think I could live in Sherwood forever."

"It was merry, wasn't it!" Marian laughed.

They left the castle, this time by the opened drawbridge, and Robin ran off toward the hill. Before he disappeared over its top, he stopped and turned around. He made a noise like a hunting owl. Marian made the same sound back. It became their signal to each other for all the time they spent in the forest. Often, in the long years when Robin was away at the Crusades, Marian would hear that sad wavering call in her restless sleep.

"Tomorrow we will shoot together," called Robin.

"And I shall show you how to find your way to the heart of Sherwood," shouted Marian, laughing.

So that is what they did. Robin of Locksley would never again be lost, for Marian became his polaris, a sharp point of light in his heart to which he turned for the rest of his life. She taught him everything she knew of the woods and her longbow. He became quite good at all of it, they say. And from that day on, Sherwood Forest was a very merry place indeed.

"What wilt thou bet, seeing our game is the worse?"
  Unto him then said Robin Hood:
"Why then," quoth the bishop, "all that's in my purse;"
  Quoth Scarlet, "That bargain is good."

—from *Robin Hood and Queen Katherine* (24)

Under the
Bending Yew

Anna Kirwan

'Twas Plough Monday. The weather was right out of the pageant of Noah we'd all seen in the square that afternoon. I was standing out in the vaporous January weather that was almost a drizzle and keeping away from my pestilence of a nephew. My older sister, Rowena, had left our parents' house in Locksley when I was a wee lad, and I know not what she was like before she married the gentleman Lud Gamwell of Blidworth, Yorkshire. But the son they made in the big oak bedstead our mother gave them is a plague to me at these family occasions.

So I hid out in the shelter of a wall where the ground rises behind the house, out under the big yew tree there. I pulled my green cloak around me and my bow and quiver and stamped my feet, and felt the wind bleating and biting my fingers. It was too cold for shooting, but I feel more myself with my bow to hand.

I pulled my green cloak around me.

I wonder about a careless lad—such as my nephew, Will—who can leave his bow behind and have to go looking for it when it's needed. I just wish't I could be back home in Barnsdale Forest.

If you wonder why Will Gamwell is such a thorn under my feathers, you might consider a few reasons. Quite a few.

His father's cloth trade is just that much richer than our Lincoln green wool brings into my father's counting room, and Will wears the difference on the corner of his smirk. Woad and gorse are good enough dyes for honest cloaks and blankets. But Will's his father's son, always talking about crimson and madder tints, and "The courtiers are paying thus much this season," and so on.

Nor is he respectful of me, his uncle and his natural elder, and—even though he was born within a twelvemonth of me—someone whose guidance he should follow. But he is a know-it-all. I would rather have stood alone out there, with suppertime coming and going, the sky grayer than a goose quill and wet as the bottom of a trough, than have to put up with his unmerry prattle.

When we rode into Blidworth, Father and Mother and I, Rowena had managed to get down to the courtyard, and to get old mulberry-spot Lud to wait there with her to pay proper attention to our father and mother. And you'd think it'd suit Gamwell Minor to be there, since they are his grandsire and granddam come to visit. But he was nowhere in evidence.

Neither was Squirrel—Marion, I mean, that tall girl, his father's ward. I'd wager, if her poor dead parents knew what her guardian's son is that they have inflicted on her, they would have thought twice about picking old Lud to be her godfather.

Squirrel is none the most meek or patient maiden, but I have always reckoned, if she dinna have to put up with so much from Will Gamwell, mayhap she wouldna always be so sharp and nibbling, so quick with the words to bite back at his provocations and puncture his bragging.

Really, she is a good deal like his mother, what with her "When wilt tha' show tha'self timely for chapel?" and "Canna tha' hush that pup o' thine?" Whene'er I've bethought me of the possibility Lud might betroth them, Will and Squirrel, it's been fair disheartening. The two of them get along no better than my sister and her husband do. With Squirrel forever scolding and Will dodging out of her way, what motley pups would they whelp? How could they not bestow another generation with another plaguey Will Gamwell?

Well, by and by, out from the green gate of the kitchen yard, here came the pestilence, dressed in madder wool and cross-garters of coral rose—a shade I'd rather see on a milkmaid's kirtle. Squirrel has a gown that color. But here was Will, in his crimson shirt and his Scarborough cloak lined in otter fur that smelt like a beach fire. No shutting him up, I guessed; he had to discuss the whole play of *Old Eezum-Squeezum and the Maw of Hell,* which the tailors' guild would be putting on that nightfall.

"Last year," he said, "there were two cutpurses came in and worked the whole town while folks stood gaping at the Noah pageant."

"Well," I said to him, "at least you must have enjoyed a profit."

"What?" says he, clearly puzzled.

40

"Why, selling new silk purses, your father's trade," I said.

Will was after giving me a sharp look. "Cutpurses," he said, "cut a leather purse first, dost not know that? Gold's too heavy to ride in a silk purse long. But watch out at the pageant tonight. No one ever caught those light-fingered throstles last year."

Something told me this was not his main inducement to seek my company in such a dismal spot. I was correct, too.

"My mother hateth me," he said then. "She desireth me to ask Squirrel to go with me. I'd rather roast my chestnuts in hell with Old Eezum."

"How, now, nephew?" I said bland and mild. "She's a worthy match. Pretty as a May tree."

"Say, rather, tall and old as a Druid oak," he grumbled. (Will is a little cockerel, after all, only up to my cheekbone.) "Old Maid Marion. I say Mother's afraid no one will have her, with her squirrel teeth, so I'm stuck."

I canna say how it amused me to hear him speak so—him, with all his spots, speckled as a trout! But it gave me leave to consider a means of comeuppance I'd not designed before.

"If some other *would* have her," I said, as easy and familiar as an old cap, just as if I were the very companion of his bosom, "sure, she'd have none but you. How could you disappoint her?"

"Well, I'll confess to it," he said then—and I saw we'd come to the meat, if not the marrow, of the matter—"I'd rather go protect Nancy Weatherstaff from the ministrations of Oxpoll, the tanner's helper. He is wide as a haystack and smells like a slop pail, and he's always looking to back her against a wall to steal kisses. Squirrel liketh me not, Robin, and she needeth me not.

41

But Nancy is such a gentle little thing." His complaint turned so sentimental and moonish, I almost laughed. "She canna stand up to Oxpoll. But I can."

I took a good look at him, then, and this was what I saw: Squirrel came to Gamwell's house, and Will was no more the apple of his mother's eye, where he had been her pride and joy. Squirrel had cut him down to size, whate'er Lud and Ro intended. She is a very minx, no question, and almost always right. I could see his point.

"Stand up to Oxpoll?" I tweaked him. "Aye, up to his knee! What can you show best at, 'gainst him?"

"Forsooth, his wit's in his hams. And if it be skill that's contested, why Uncle, tha' taught me tha'self to shoot. I can silence any who'll put his argument in a bull's-eye. Even God's own Maypole, Marion, would wager as much."

Then did something occur I'd not foreseen. The dank branches of the yew above us did quake and creak and swear oaths as scarlet as Will's garments.

"Watch out, then, tha' libelous carbuncle!" a voice called down on us, and Squirrel dropped out of the yew like a crab from a crab tree. "I'll show thee 'God's Maypole,' that I shall! As to tha' bull's-eye—I'd not lay such a wager, tha' squeaking blister. I've seen tha' Uncle Robin Hode shoot—who's the better there, eh? 'Squirrel's teeth,' is't? Look to what tha' has that they might bite!"

"Squirrel, girl," quoth Will then—and here's the silk of him, that he showed neither riled nor worried—"I do but idly speak. Be not wrathful wi' me."

42

"Nay, tha' boast tha' aim and arm. That's one sin. And tha' hast scant courtesy—that's another." She leant over him as if she were a steeple like to topple. "Look thee at tha' uncle, standing here in the mist to hear thee! Poor Robin, with no more wel-come than this! Where art tha' kindly manners, Will? Give him tha' shirt to warm the heart that taught thee, as tha' boast, to shoot so well."

He gave her a look as glum and black as Old Eezum's bile, but he did it. He took off his overshirt and gave it to me to pay penalty for speaking so discourteously—behind her back, as it were, though, in sooth, 'twas beneath her feet. (The shirt fitteth me well, only the sleeves are short. I may ask someone to cut it down to a tunic of some different style lest it be said I wear his castoffs.)

"You think your dusty longbow will bend fair enow to such a contest to take the prize?" I asked him then. "You must be bet-ter at it than last I saw you. But you'll shame the family if you judge ill. Let's see a shot hit a mark. Here, Marion," I said as sweetly as 'twas in me. "You shall set the task for this braggart re-lation of mine." Looking about the garden sweepings and mid-den near the gate, my eye fell on a discard sprig of holly tied with a scrap of red ribbon. "Set this up where you choose," I bid her. "We'll see who has the skill to steal a prize from another."

"She ne'er so much as nocked an arrow, herself," Will protested. "How can she place a target reasonably?"

"Tha' quibbling fleabite," Squirrel dressed him, "I'm like to place it on the fat bagpipes of tha' vanity, and watch thee flinch and shrivel." But she grinned at me, then darted out toward a cluster of rowan trees at least thirty yards away.

43

Now, I had thought to humble Will once for all in this match, but as soon as Squirrel was away from us, he spoke urgently under his breath.

"Uncle, I *have* improved my aim, see if I haven't. But here's a wager I lay before you. If I shoot better than you in this test, say you'll take the sour wench to the pageant as if 'twere your own desire. But let her not know 'tis a penalty."

The plague on it—his conceit is swollen like a leech left on too long! But my mother's counsel hath taught me to forswear impatience.

"On such a slender thread you'd wager?" I chided him mildly. My wits were circling like a juggler's beanbags. "If Squirrel sees you win to lose her, you will have popped from the griddle to the flame," I reminded him. "And anyway, you know I'll win my shot."

But Will look't out at the wee holly sprig Squirrel had pegged to the farthest rowan trunk, and then he look't me squarely in the eye and said, "I know nowt o' that. I shoot to win my heart's true wish, Uncle. I'll let it rest at that and trust tha' words to cool her spleen. Look, she returneth anon. Is it a wager?"

I shrugged. Anything to shut him up and be rid of him, I told myself.

Squirrel was back, then, the drops of mist hanging on her brown hair like a silver net. I call her "Squirrel" because it's what she's called, yet there's nowt to her looks wherein I'd find fault. She's had the name since she was a little maiden, methinks. She must have grown into her teeth, for they are neat in her grin now, white as altar linen. Our Lady couldna have a prettier smile, though I doubt Our Lady would wink at a lad the way Squirrel winked at me when she returned from the rowans.

"Hit that," she said to Will, "tha' trembling, ruddy jelly." He *was* shivering, with only his linen undershirt beneath his cloak. But I dinna feel sorry for him. I have no cloak lined in otter.

I handed over to him my bow and sheath of arrows.

"They're dry for now," I told him. "Take aim quickly, though, or 'twill be a fish shoot."

I could tell from the look he gave me as he took them that he'd feigned his sure confidence. For all his puffed-up talk, he's none foolish, Will Gamwell. He knows he's not the only one as practices his aim. He flexed the bow to test its spring, and he plucked the string to gauge its music, and he pulled three arrows out from the quiver and carefully sighted along them before choosing the one he liked best.

He drew his eyebrows together, and I could see the blacks of his eyes flutter. He was just about to shoot when Squirrel said, "Nancy Weatherstaff. The dairy maid, by God's dog!"

"Nay, Marion," I said, making bold to lay a hand on her pink sleeve—and I will not say anything as to how I felt at that touch. " 'Tis a fair trial you've set him. Let him do his best."

I stood a few paces behind him and stooped over a bit so I could watch how he sighted. He nocked the shaft afresh, then, and drew back the string—and shot. The shaft made hardly a sound in the wet air, not so much as a drop sizzling on a griddle. But it skewered the waving tag of scarlet ribbon.

"There!" he cried. "At this distance! See! There's no better shot this afternoon, tha' knows it!"

45

"Hush," Squirrel cut him off. "Give that lot to me, tha' mole, don't even disturb Robin." Suddenly, she was well annoyed with him again.

And, by my soul, she took my bow right out of his hand!

"I'll give you 'never nocked'! How dare you?" she chided. "*I'll* give you a better shot!"

"I canna keep up with you, Marion," Will mumbled uncomfortably. " 'Don't tell,' you said. 'Don't tell anyone I've been shooting at targets, like a lad.' "

But she pushed her own cloak off her sweet shoulder and took pretty quick aim and, by all the saints, she got the other tail of the ribbon on the holly!

She is one of a kind, Squirrel is, matchless as girls occur.

"Tha'd set tha'self against Oxpoll?" she taunted. "Tha' canna prove tha'self nor better nor a maiden of scant education."

"Stay your scorn and your bickering," I spoke up then. I had my idea. "Let me shoot now mine own bow and third-truest arrow, and talk after."

Will's face was a study, whether it showed more abashed or hopeful. When he is shut up and not bragging, he is young for his age, I think.

I shot, and my arrow hit a straggling holly leaf.

"That was what I aimed at," I said.

"Fie, tha' fibber!" Will laughed.

"By courtesy, you gave us your good, dry darts," Squirrel realized. She looked prettily baffled—and 'tisn't a way one sees her ofttimes.

46

"Make not excuses for him," Will urged cheerily. "Another day he'll do better."

The cheeky little ferret! He shall be taught humility some day, I vow.

"If you have no more honor than that," I said calmly, "take your prize and go to the pageant as you like, and disregard me, your uncle."

"If you think I'd go in public with such a vain, piping chick, you think foolishness," Squirrel declared with some passion. "Go, throw tha'self at Nancy's dainty buskins!"

Will looked at me, astonished and grateful. Then, no doubt afraid I'd blink and he'd be in trouble again, he was off through the gate. He did not even ask for his shirt back—I'd have given it, but he didn't ask. He has others.

When he was gone, the mist dripped quietly about Squirrel and me. I did hear a bullfinch, off to the west of us, and a gabble of moorhens farther away. Squirrel dinna seem to know what to say. But it was finally she that broke silence.

"How say you, then, Robin?" she asked courteously.

"You gave away too much, lady," I said, as sweet as was in me. "You took your shot when you'd seen only one arrow in the weather. But you let me watch two. We're well rid of Will Gamwell for awhile, though."

Then I nocked another arrow—and *all* my arrows are true— and put it through the knot of the bow, right through, so my arrow had a lip of ribbon all around it.

Squirrel was impressed.

Robyn bent a full goode bowe,
An arrowe he drowe at wyll;
He hit so the proude sherife
Upon the grounde he lay full still.

Robin bent a very good bow,
An arrow he drew at will;
He so hit the proud sheriff
That upon the ground he lay quite still.

—from *A Gest of Robyn Hode*
sixth fytte six (347)

Know Your True Enemy

Nancy Springer

"Will we kill him?" Rafe whispered, his heart beating hard.

"Shhh," breathed Little John by way of answer, though there was not much need for silence. The great ramping horse, caparisoned in the Nottingham colors, was well and truly caught in ivy, vines as strong as a hangman's noose. Rafe grimly smiled at the sight; when would these brass-helmeted, high-horse men at arms learn that their mighty mounts were useless in the forest? Atop the steed, the rider struggled to throw off the clinging vines. There was little fear that he would escape before—

Revenge! The word was less a thought than a heat burning in Rafe's veins. For a sixmonth he had been a wolf's head, an outlaw with Robin in Sherwood who could be killed by anyone for a reward, just as a wolf could be killed for bounty. But this was the first time he had stalked toward revenge, longbow in hand.

Two more silent steps and he stood by Little John's side with lifted bow, waiting for Robin's signal.

It came—a birdlike whistle, mocking and cheery. Rafe stepped forward; a dozen outlaws stepped forward at once, bows drawn, ringing the rider with razor-sharp steel arrowpoints.

The rider startled like a deer. A stray branch caught at his helmet; it fell off.

Then Robin lowered his bow and began to laugh.

From atop the frothing horse, the rider glared at the outlaws. Rafe saw dark eyes in a thin, pale face. Narrow shoulders. Arms like sticks, and skinny hands trembling on the reins.

"By my troth, it's a boy!" Robin cried.

A stripling. Almost as tall as a man but no more than twelve years old. "What are you doing on that horse, lad?" Little John inquired.

"I know him," said another outlaw. "It's the sheriff's son."

Rafe's grip tightened on his bow. But other outlaws laughed or meowed like catbirds. Someone cried, "Oooh! On papa's horse? Watch out, sonny. Papa will spank."

"Come on." Robin stepped forward and started cutting the ivy away with his long hunting knife. Others helped. Little John, standing more than six feet tall, reached up to lift vines away from the rider, but the youngster pulled back from him.

"Get your foul hands off of me!" Those were the first words he had spoken, and he failed to make them manly; his voice cracked and squeaked. Robin chuckled and joined Little John,

51

the two of them untangling the boy and lifting him off the horse. "I do not yield!" he cried, thrashing against them. He wore a short sword but did not think to reach for it; he just squirmed and flailed. "Let me go!" he yelled. "You let me go, or my father will punish you."

"Spitfire!" Robin exclaimed, grinning, as they laid him on the ground and took the sword away. "What are we going to do with him, merry men?"

"Spank him and send him back to his papa!"

"Hold him for ransom."

"Hold him hostage."

"Give him a Sherwood Forest welcome!"

"Kill him," said Rafe, who had not moved from his place through all this. He had lowered his bow, but he gripped it so tightly that his fist shook.

Robin gave him a quiet, level glance. There was understanding in that glance but also warning. "We do not kill children," Robin said.

Rafe said nothing more, but he glared at the boy on the ground more fiercely than the boy glared at the outlaws. A child? But the youngster was not much younger than Rafe himself. How could Robin call this snot nose a child? Rafe was not much taller, not much stronger, not much older, yet he knew himself to be a man.

"My father will find me. My father will come and save me and kill all of you."

Rafe was getting mightily tired of hearing this, but Robin just smiled. "Quite so. Certainly," he replied affably to the captive. "But we'll just keep you for the sake of your charming company meanwhile. Are you sure you won't have some mead?"

The sheriff's son shook his head. The outlaws were indeed giving him a Sherwood Forest welcome, feasting on the king's deer and washing the venison down with mead, but the guest of honor just sat in his place by the campfire and glowered. They had fresh-baked bread also (received in uneven trade for a fine horse) and butter, but the sheriff's son would not eat. He would not tell them his name. He would not say why he was in the forest. He would say only, "My father will save me."

Even the honey mead tasted bitter to Rafe that night. He went early to his deerskin shelter and his bed.

Little John woke him for his turn at watch a couple of hours before daybreak. Robin had set more than the usual watch, Rafe found. There was not much fear that the Sheriff of Nottingham could find Robin's camp—he had been trying for years—but the gods might favor him more now, with his son gone. Curse the proud brat. Rafe kept careful watch.

"He's gone!"

The sunrise yell from the main tent jerked Rafe's head around. It couldn't be. Not on his watch.

But it was.

Gone. They had given the sheriff's son a blanket in the middle of the tent to sleep on, and they hadn't tied him—he was just a boy, and he'd awaken one of them if he tried to go anywhere, they reasoned. Perhaps the mead hadn't helped their reasoning as much as it had helped their slumber.

"Did no one see or hear *anything?*" Robin chided the guards.

Rafe bit his lip and could not reply. Neither did anyone else. After a moment Little John said in his quiet, gentle way, "They were watching for Nottingham to come in, Robin. Not for the lad to slip out."

"Well, fan out, men. Find him."

"Break camp," Little John suggested, "if you're thinking the boy will bring a hornet's nest down on us."

"It's not that. I'm afraid he'll come to harm. He's afoot, he has no idea where he is, and he doesn't know how to fend for himself in the woods. He's likely to starve if we don't find him."

"Let him starve!" Rafe burst out.

Robin gave him a long look. "Know your true enemy, Rafe," he said at last, without anger. "And meanwhile, do as I say. Go now."

Rafe did it, he set out to search, but his feelings rode hard and heavy in his empty belly. Come to harm indeed; had the sheriff's son cared when good men came to harm at his father's hands? The brat was devil get. Let him come to harm.

Sometimes Rafe did not understand Robin at all.

With his lips tightened into a line like a bowstring, he slipped through the forest, edging his way between thorn thickets and rocky scarps and the great grandfather oaks. He stayed away from the trails made by deer and less fortunate wanderers; outlaws knew better than to follow trails. But when he came upon a trail, he ghosted along to one side of it, checking for the boy.

After a moment, Little John said in his quiet, gentle way . . .

He reached the edge of a rocky gorge and stood still, scanning the stream at the bottom of the ravine in case the brat might have gone there for water.

"Rafe."

The soft voice made him jump as if prodded by a spear. He spun around, crouching to fight—and looked straight into the eyes of the sheriff's son.

Huddled against the damp belly of a boulder, the youngster looked levelly back at him, his dark eyes like a shot deer's. His pale face glistened with moisture, his hunched shoulders trembled. Rafe's breath caught in his chest—on the boy's jerkin and leggings he saw brown blotches of blood. Just below the right knee, half-hidden by dried leaves, clung a great cold arc of steel.

Mantrap.

SNAP. Saw-toothed jaws sharp and heavy enough to kill a wolf. Or a wolf's head. Meant to harm as well as to hold.

The sheriff's men had set it where the trail narrowed, dropping to the gorge, passing between a beech and the boulder, where the leaves that hid the steel would naturally gather. They would not be back to check on it for another month or two. Hoping to find the moldering skeleton of some outlaw.

The boy's leg was badly mangled. Broken.

It took Rafe a moment to come to grips with all this. Once before he had seen someone caught in a mantrap, and the memory burned through him. *Revenge.* It gave him all the more reason to wish the sheriff's son dead. Such fitting justice. The sheriff's own son dead in the sheriff's vile trap.

He could turn and leave. No one had to learn he had ever found the brat.

He felt the boy's gaze on him. He felt the stricken, trembling pain in that gaze, but even more, he felt the silence. It was as if the youngster knew what he was thinking.

Proud brat. He did not beg. He did not speak. He had spoken only a single word.

Rafe.

He had called him by name. How did he know his name?

Rafe let out a long, shaky breath and swallowed hard. Then he lifted his head, put his fingers to his teeth and whistled. He knew from before that he could not open the trap by himself. His alarm signal rose wavering at first, then high and clear, as shrill as a hawk's scream.

Then he knelt beside the sheriff's son. "Don't you know how to shout?" he grumbled, pulling off his deerskin tunic and wrapping it around the boy's shivering shoulders. "Why didn't you call out? Did you plan to sit here until you died?"

The sheriff's son was brave, Rafe admitted to himself. The boy had not cried out when they had pried the trap open. Death white, he had made no sound as they lifted him out and carried him back to camp. He was not crying out now, with Rafe holding him down and Robin and Little John peeling the bloody wrappings away from his mangled leg.

Kneeling on the ground by the sheriff's son, Robin said, "Find him something to bite, Rafe."

Rafe undid his hunting knife from his belt and placed it, tough leather sheath and all, between the boy's teeth. There was blood on the boy's lower lip; he had bitten it. Robin had noticed.

"It's a clean break," Robin told the sheriff's son, hand on the boy's leg. "We'll set it as quickly as we can."

Knees on the boy's shoulders, hands leaning on his arms, Rafe felt him shaking.

"Ready?" Robin said to Little John. "Now."

The boy tried not to struggle, Rafe could tell, but "brave" can only do so much. The boy arched his back, straining, writhing. He screamed—by all the world's suffering, how he screamed—then went limp. Rafe closed his eyes.

Why had Robin chosen him for this? It was almost cruel.

"Thank the gods he's fainted," Robin murmured. "Brandy, Rafe."

Wobbling, Rafe went to fetch the bottle. When he returned, he knelt by the sheriff's son and started to pour some between the boy's slack lips.

"Not for him," Robin said. "We want him to stay the way he is for a while. It's for us, lad. Have some."

Later, as they were wrapping the last binding around the splints, the sheriff's son moaned, stiffened, and opened his eyes.

"What's your name, son?" Robin asked him gently.

He whispered, "It's—it's Tod."

"Tod. It's a good name for you. You're a proper young fox, giving us the slip."

They laid him to a soft bed of furs. Rafe brought a fresh jerkin,

57

and Robin started to unlace Tod's ruined one. The hurt boy seemed not to realize at first what was going on, but then he tried to pull back. "Don't."

"Just trying to get this bloody, sweaty thing"—Robin stripped it away—"off of you—"

Robin faltered to silence, staring at the boy's skinny body—his narrow shoulders striped with welts, his bony ribs mottled with fresh dark bruises.

Between clenched teeth Robin breathed, "Who has done this to you?"

Tod said nothing.

"Your father?"

"He—he beats me only to toughen me."

The look on Robin's face made Rafe step forward and slip the clean jerkin onto Tod, hiding the marks.

Robin found his voice. "That makes as much sense as stripping the bark off a young tree. To toughen it."

Tod closed his eyes and turned away. "Hush, Robin," Little John said gruffly. "The lad needs food and sleep, not a lecture."

Robin demanded, "Does he 'toughen' your mother, too?"

"Robin." Little John reached out a huge callused hand and urged Robin out of the tent. Rafe was left sitting by the bedside of the sheriff's son.

"My father will come looking for me," Tod said. "My father will find me."

"Taking his time, isn't he?" Rafe teased. Three times Robin's band had broken camp and followed the deer through Sherwood

Forest since the day they found Tod. It had been a full turn of the moon and a fortnight more, with no sign of the Sheriff of Nottingham.

"Likely he's got important matters to attend to," Tod said. "With the king."

The boy spoke of his father less often as time went by, as he roamed camp on the crutches Little John had made him, pestering everyone, learning how to stitch a belt or skin a deer or fletch an arrow. He had to be feeling poorly to be talking about his father now, Rafe knew. Rafe stirred the soup and stopped teasing. "That's it. No doubt about it." He put a stick of wood on the small campfire, then sat down by Tod and offered another stick, a green one. "You want to whittle a point on that? In case Little John brings back a rabbit?"

The thought that he could do something for Little John helped the boy, as Rafe knew it would. Tod smiled and reached—

A whistle as shrill as a hawk's scream soared over Sherwood Forest.

Rafe leaped to his feet, snatching for his bow. Tod scrambled for his crutches and struggled up, though he had heard that signal only once before—for his own sake. Robin sprinted past, running in the direction from which the alarm had come, gone in an eye blink as the forest hid him.

Rafe's mind squirreled; he could barely think what to do. "Help me put out the fire." He scattered blazing sticks with his booted foot, and he and Tod stamped the flames away. "Come." He started off with Tod crutching after him.

Slow. Making his way through the forest as quickly as he could, the boy was still so slow that Rafe felt half wild with waiting for him. His heart pounded with fear—what had happened? Was someone hurt?

He did not say that maybe Tod's father had come for him at last. Neither did Tod.

"Go—ahead," Tod puffed. "I'll—catch up."

Rafe wanted to. He wanted to be with the others, not babysitting this boy. He knew that Tod was likely to get lost in the forest if he left, but—but what if he were missing a chance to help Robin? What if just one more hand were needed, what if he, Rafe, could be the man who saved—

Tod's crutch tip caught on a root, and he pitched forward, sprawling in the dirt. Rafe pressed his lips together, bent to help him up, and saw another hand reach down. He had not heard so much as one leaf rustling, but there stood Robin.

"Come, lad. On my back." Robin hoisted Tod and strode off. Rafe grabbed Tod's crutches and trotted after them.

"What has happened?" Tod asked before Rafe could.

Robin did not answer. And glancing at Robin's face, seeing his hard jaw and his shadowed eyes, Rafe did not dare to press the question.

Tod asked, "Robin?"

"Tod, lad." Robin spoke gently to him, as usual. "Tell me: The day we first found you on that great, ramping horse, what were you doing? Were you running away from your father?"

It was a question the boy had always turned aside. But this

time, hearing Robin's quiet, serious voice, Tod seemed to know that he had to answer, and answer truly.

"In a way. But not the way you mean." Tod took a deep breath. "I wanted to—to find an outlaw. To please him. To make him proud of me."

Please don't laugh, the boy's face begged. But Robin showed no sign of merriment, and Rafe did not feel like laughing either.

"I see," Robin said. Rafe saw also, or remembered: a boy on a man's horse, trying to be a man—to please the Sheriff of Nottingham.

Robin strode along rapidly and silently for some time, with Rafe half-running to stay by his side. Finally Robin said, "Tod. Suppose I were to tell you it's time for you to go home. What would you say?"

"Why?" The boy's voice wavered. "What has happened?"

"I'm thinking of exchanging you as a hostage, lad." Robin's level voice had gone as taut as a stretched leather shield, and Rafe looked at him in a new way: Sometimes Robin had to make difficult decisions, too.

"Why? Who—"

"Your father has captured Little John."

At the edge of the forest near Nottingham the outlaws had gathered, their lips tight, their hands tight on their bows, not speaking as their leader joined them.

"Anything?" Robin asked. The high road to Nottingham curved near Sherwood at that point. As Rafe understood it,

Little John had been taken by a patrol on sortie to the north. The sheriff would come riding—

"Soon." The lookout jerked his chin at a puff of dust growing nearer. Rafe heard the trampling of horses, harsh voices, saw the glint of brazen helms. And the sheriff's breastplate—on a heavy-headed charger the sheriff rode in the fore.

Then Rafe saw Little John. Afoot, stumbling, being jerked along by the rope that bound his arms. Rafe could see blood on his face, and his stomach knotted; he felt as if he himself had been struck.

Tod might expect to be beaten when he returned home. But Little John might expect to be hanged at dawn.

"Lad?" said Robin to Tod.

Staring at Little John, the boy swallowed hard, then nodded and crutched forward. Weaponless, Robin walked with him. Rafe took his place with the others, his hands trembling upon his ready bow.

Tod stood in the middle of the road with Robin beside him as his father rounded the curve—and saw him.

Hand on the boy's shoulder, Robin called, "Sheriff!"

It was the signal. The merry men stepped forward, just out of their leafy cover, presenting a score of arrows nocked to fly. Nottingham yanked his charger to a halt, his armor jangling, and his patrol stopped behind him.

"An exchange of prisoners, Sheriff, if you please," said Robin.

Staring at Tod, the sheriff barely blinked. His meaty face creased and he roared with angry laughter. "That runt?" He laughed. "That scrawny wretch? He's useless. Keep him. Do with him what you will. If you live long enough." He lifted a gauntleted hand in sudden angry command. "Slay the wolf's head!"

Robin lunged for the side of the road, taking Tod with him, shielding the boy with his body as the first volley of arrows flew. Then he snatched up Tod and ran for the forest.

Rafe loosed his bolt, terrified of hitting Little John—but Little John had stepped behind one of the horses, knowing what was about to happen—and then it was all dust and yells and the sound of his own heartbeat pounding and hooves pounding toward him and he was too young and too scared and he couldn't get the next arrow to nock straight—

"Help Tod!" Robin yelled in his ear, grabbing the bow out of his hand.

Rafe almost stumbled over the boy a few paces behind him. His crutches lost, Tod crawled, clung to a tree to pull himself upright, tried to hobble away. Rafe hoisted him in his arms as best he could and ran. His gut did not argue against Robin's orders this time.

He had carried the boy not quite far enough for safety when he had to stop. The pain in his chest would let him go no farther. Panting, he let Tod slip to the ground and felt the boy's chest heaving worse than his own.

Tears on the boy's face. Tod was crying.

Rafe folded beside him and gathered him into his arms.

"Bloody hell," Tod whispered, huddled against his chest, trying to stop sobbing.

Rafe swallowed hard and held him, stroking his back. Listening to the sounds of battle not quite far enough away. Listening to the sounds, nearer at hand, of a boy turning into a man.

Tod quieted. Rafe's panting eased. The yells and screams went on. Rafe got up to take Tod to safety, lifting the boy with him.

"I can walk," Tod said, his voice almost steady.

Rafe set him on his feet and walked beside him. Tod hung onto him with one hand and hobbled along.

They left the sounds of battle behind them, walking in silence broken only by the soft comments of ringdoves and beech leaves.

"Rafe," Tod asked, his voice low, "did Robin have a father who—who cared for him?"

Rafe had never thought of Robin that way. It was hard to think of Robin with a father, hard to think of him as a child. "I don't know."

"Did you? Did you have a father who—" Tod faltered, trying to voice the concept of fatherly love.

"Yes."

"But he—he's dead?"

"Yes."

"How?"

Rafe clenched his teeth. He did not want to answer.

"Rafe?"

He stopped walking, and Tod stopped beside him. The sheriff's son was almost his height; he had to stoop only slightly to face him levelly. Keeping his voice as gentle as the voices of ringdoves and leaves, Rafe said, "Your father killed him."

In a mantrap. But Rafe did not say that.

Tod's eyes widened as if he had just taken an arrow to the

heart. Rafe could not face that grief, mirror of his own. He had to turn away. "Come on."

They walked.

Halfway back to camp, Tod said, "That's why you didn't like me at first."

"Yes."

"But you don't hate me anymore."

"No." Know your true enemy, Robin had said, and Rafe knew it now.

Tod lifted his hand in a last farewell, then turned his horse and sent it cantering away from the forest.

From the shelter of a mighty oak, Rafe and Robin lifted their hands in response, then watched after him until he disappeared over a barley-covered hilltop.

"It's what he has to do," Robin said, maybe to still his own doubts and fears. Rafe had said nothing. "He's too young to be branded a wolf's head."

"But for him to ride that distance by himself . . ." Tod was riding toward the holdings of his mother's people, several leagues to the east. And if they tried to send him back to his father, he would ride on to the king's court in London. Perhaps the king would give him justice. Rafe ached with worry for Tod riding alone through a dangerous land—but there was nothing Rafe could do to help; Robin needed him. Robin and the band. They had rescued Little John, but at the cost of three dead, four wounded.

And they had captured a horse and given it to Tod to send him on his way.

"He will be all right," Robin said. "He is a proper young fox, remember?"

Rafe nodded, remembering how he had wished Tod dead the day Robin had first called Tod that. Robin was too good to say it, but Rafe knew that he was thinking the same: Know your true enemy.

Rafe knew it, and it was his own hatred.

Silently he and Robin turned, slipping back into the forest. Overhead, a hawk screamed.

We live here like squires, or lords of renown,
*   Without ere a foot of free land;*
We feast on good cheer, with wine, ale, and beer,
*   And evry thing at our command.*

Then musick and dancing did finish the day;
*   At length, when the sun waxed low,*
Then all the whole train the grove did refrain
*   And unto their caves they did go.*

—from *Robin Hood and Little John* (37–38)

THE CHILDREN'S WAR

Timons Esaias

Four of the king's rabbits, fat enough to roast, filled Niam's little game sack. He had just reset the last snare when the ground shook through his heels.

His playmate, Lewis, whispered, "Horses!" and scurried to the lookout spot. By the time he got back Niam had already tied the bag tight and cleaned his small dagger. The dagger once belonged to a sergeant of the Nottingham Guard. It would mean death to be caught with it.

Lewis's hand gesture meant "enemy riders coming into the forest." Niam followed him along a narrow path to the place where they had set a mantrap months before.

Taking his own position, Niam waited for the signal from Lewis. After scaling up the trunk of a big mossy elm, Lewis

"Horses!"

would be peering along the narrow sight line the boys had cleared of leaves and branches three times this year already.

A leaden shot, a rough ball hammered out of some stolen roofing sheets by one of the old men, rested high in another tree. Tied up in netting, it had two vines attached to it. A thick vine ran from the shot to another tree. This thick vine was the one the heavy shot would swing down on. It would swoop along the path just above saddle height. God willing, it would kill a sheriff's man or two this day.

The second vine, much thinner, ran from the shot to Niam's hiding place. With it, he would pull the shot off its resting place to begin its plunge.

Niam pulled the slack out of the slender vine. He could hear the patrol approaching at a jog trot. His thigh muscles began cramping from anticipation.

Too excited, he tried to crane his neck to see the path himself and at first didn't recognize Lewis's woodpecker signal. It was repeated, louder the second time, and he felt his face blush red with shame. Then he pulled the vine with all his strength. He felt the weight of the shot leave the end of his vine, and he saw the main vine slicing through the branches. Twigs snapped, leaves fluttered loose, and a *swoosh* sounded above the drumming of hooves and the ringing of saddle gear.

He saw Lewis step out onto a branch for a clearer view, when a quick succession of sounds pulled Niam's attention away. A shout, horses startling, and a couple of dull thuds. Immediately he knew the trap had gone wrong. The thuds were the shot hitting the ground rather than armor or flesh. It had the sound of a nine-pins ball, bowled on pebbly soil.

Just as Niam turned to run—as fast and as far as ever he could—Lewis dropped out of the tree in front of him. His friend had a funny shocked grin on his face. He also had an arrow through his arm.

"Stupid child!" Niam's mother screamed, despite the four plump rabbits. "Idiot child!" she screamed as she slashed at him with a herding switch of peeled willow. It tore into his forearm and laid the flesh open. "My own child," she moaned as she gently bound up the wound afterward and put a plaster on it to keep out disease.

The other names she called him kept burning in his mind for weeks.

Lewis almost had it better. The shaft of the horseman's arrow had come out cleanly. Now he could nobly recount how he had been wounded in battle, and how, even if he never bent the arm again, he would avenge himself upon the cowardly soldiers and their vile Plantagenet king. The men, the merry men, laughed. But they laughed pleasantly.

Niam hid the wound his mother gave him under a raw deer-hide armguard and avoided the jeering questions of the other children. Unfairly, they had decided the botched ambush was his fault.

One of the uncles had inspected the ground and described the outcome of the encounter on the road. "Looks like the netting the boys put around the lead had rotted some. It tore out and hit the roadbed and bounced a couple of times." One horse had been found nearby, its harness stripped, its off-foreleg shattered and dangling.

The whole camp had eaten horse stew for two days.

"Children ambushing a king's patrol!" some women scornfully snapped. The men laughed uncomfortably then, for they knew that most of the children in the camp had done the same already. It was the children who had infested the forest's edge with mantraps, and caltrops to hurt the horses, and horse-leg pits and swinging traps. And children who left secret markers so that poor locals, poaching and stealing firewood in the Great Forest, would not run afoul of the dangers. Rarely, now, did Robin's men fight directly with the sheriff's reluctant troops. But just as rarely did a week pass without one of these same soldiers wounded or worse by the children's war.

His father's displeasure surprised Niam. His mother was British, and some said that was why she had a fierce and flaring temper. But John Freeman, his freehold farm taken by the Norman rulers, had been one of the first Saxon freemen to put on the Lincoln green and follow Robin into the forest. Niam had heard a hundred times how John Freeman had stood by Robin in several battles and once helped drag the wounded leader out of a desperate situation. Three great scars across his father's chest, faded white with passing years, marked the event.

John Freeman was John Weaver now, having learned to fashion reed baskets while living with this outlaw band. They couldn't do much farming in Sherwood Forest. Even the sheriff's men, poor soldiers though they were, could find a plowed field.

John Weaver listened to Lewis's tale, and his brow grew dark with anger. "The children are becoming outlaws!" he said. He spat into the fire, then, and Niam knew he only spat when he was very upset indeed.

Another man chuckled and said that it was ". . . natural, boys following the trade of their fathers. Apprenticed outlaws, that's what they are. All of them."

John Weaver let the conversation roll on for a while, but then he spat into the fire again. "I came into these woods free. Only King John and his sheriff said I was an outlaw. Same as most of you." No one spoke, as John Weaver tried to frame his next words. "These boys are becoming the outlaws we only pretend to be."

Niam lost patience when the grown-ups talked as if they were just town folks with town folks' manners and graces, as if they weren't hunted criminals with a price on every one of their heads. They *were* outlaws—everybody knew it—and trying to put a different face on it didn't make any sense to him. But he did know his father was disappointed in him.

Tom Fletcher had an arrow-making workshop in an old mine, there between the River Poulter and the Maun, which the sheriff's men would never discover. The entrance was just a narrow shaft, like an abandoned well, but at the bottom, one crawled along a tunnel into a big room. And there were other rooms beyond that one, connected by long passages. In the weeks following the ambush, Niam spent most of his time down there.

Niam helped Tom straighten arrows and talked to him while he sharpened the steel arrowheads. Tom seemed to like the company when there was real work to do, but he wasn't as busy as he used to be, or so he said. They used arrows for hunting here in the forest but not often for battle. Sometimes they sold bundles of them, but well to the west at the Chester Fair or up into Scotland. "We wouldn't want the sheriff buying them, now would we, lad?"

It was dry in the mine, and two of the rooms were stacked with lumber for arrows and for bows, smelling forever of yew and birch and maple. Farther back was a room filled with crossbows, neglected and rusting slowly. These had all been taken from king's men, over the years. But Robin's men never used these weapons, which were more fit for castle guards and for big battles on open battlefields. Here in the forest they shot the simple Saxon bow; though a few of them, and Robin himself, favored the British longbow.

Tom set Niam to oiling and polishing the crossbows one day, when there didn't seem to be anything else to do. It was boring work, and lonely in the isolated room with only one small oil lamp for light. But no one was making fun of him there, and he could daydream without any adults complaining.

His father seemed to complain about everything Niam did. Niam's attention wandered too much when slicing reeds, and his fingers were never nimble enough to be trusted with baskets—or so his father said. "All the boy's good for is chopping and gathering," was his opinion.

Niam liked the feel of these bows and the heft of the heavy

bolts in the hand. A fascinating mechanism bent the flexible iron bow back, and another released it with a simple flick of a trigger. The men called them boys' weapons because there were no tired arms from holding a bent bow while waiting for the right moment to let fly; and no patient practice learning how to release the arrow without sending it astray. You just pointed it and shot.

Niam also liked the ingenuity of the bolts these bows could shoot. Some of them ended in big arrowheads just like hunting arrows. Others had lead knobs at the head for knocking a man down or out of the saddle. Some held little reservoirs for tar, which could be lit to make fire arrows that were harder to put out than the straw flares most archers used for fire. Many of them had whistles cast into the head, so they would scream as they flew. These were used for battle signals and also to frighten the enemy's horses.

In his daydreams, Niam proved to everyone that he was the bravest and the most daring of the merry men. He conquered the sheriff's minions at every turn. He could kill with a sword in one hand and a bow in the other, the arrow pulled back in his teeth.

Even in his daydreams, though, in a practical part of his mind, he knew that fighting was dangerous. No matter how fast you nocked each arrow, an enemy might shoot back or stab or lance before you killed him. And no bow could shoot more than a couple of arrows at once. He dreamed of ways to shoot faster than anyone, strike with a mace in each hand, or carry two swords or two shields, but he never really had enough hands to make the dreams convincing.

Then, one warm morning when the rain came only in fine

spurts, as he looked for new places to put rabbit snares, he came across a broken pie cart. A little thing meant to be drawn by a goat or a child or a dog.

"What's that the lads have got there? Don't get that in our way, sons, unless you've really got pies in there, then," said one of the men who were practicing their archery in the Ant Meadow Butts. The big ant mounds, some of them taller than a man and bigger than two oxen, made good targets that didn't break the arrows or dull the points too much.

Just as they had practiced it several times in the preceding days, Niam and Lewis calmly wheeled the cart around, pointing the back of it toward the nearest target mound. Then, with a single yank they pulled off the canvas cover to reveal not pies but crossbows attached to each of the pie shelves. Lewis held the cart rods up, aiming all the bows at once, and Niam shot them as quick as his young fingers could trip the triggers.

The men, just as Niam had hoped—better than Niam had hoped—stood stunned as sixteen heavy bolts battered the target in less time than they could get off a second shot.

All morning long the two boys repeated the performance. Men, and women, too, came down to the Ant Meadow and watched them loose storm after storm of screaming bolts against the targets. Old Much Millersson came down; and so did Robin's fancy-dressing, clever-tongued cousin, Will Scarlet. "What a thing for an ambush!" exclaimed the men between themselves. "What a thing to clear out a sally port!" others replied.

Robin himself rode in and watched the performance just once. He pushed his horse through the spectators and asked Tom Fletcher, "Tom, how many crossbows are there still in storage?"

"I scarcely know anymore, there being no call for them. But young Niam there has been tending them."

"Well, lad?"

"Five score at least, my lord," said Niam, who had never, ever spoken to Robin before in his life.

A flicker of displeasure crossed the man's features at the "my lord," but then they softened. "This is a fine contrivance, young sirs. A fine contrivance, indeed."

Before he rode off he begged Tom Fletcher to round up some carters and fashion as many of these engines as they had bows for.

There were kind congratulations from grown men, manly claps on the shoulder, and respectful cuffs to the head. There were more demonstrations. The day would have been perfect, but it ended up entirely spoiled.

For Niam's father was there, suddenly, watching the shooting and scowling mightily. He said nothing, but shook his head, spat, and disappeared toward the camp.

"Yer father's a coward, is what it is," snipped Lewis, who would now be in charge of the cart they had built. "He's a plain coward."

The other children, jealous of the praise Niam had received, were meaner. "Your father's a coward, and you are, too!"

And despite his fury Niam could not answer them except with childish curses. They must be right about his father, for why else would the family be leaving Sherwood Forest? The Weavers had bought an old cart and were settling debts and packing all their belongings—Father set and determined, Mother busy and upset. His parents spoke civilly enough to the neighbors, but not at all to Niam except to give him the next chore and the next and the next.

Some folks laughed at them, some made jokes from across the camp. Things like "Wot? Going to visit your place in the country?" or "Cheap venison's not good enough for some, nor free firewood neither." Niam's mother put her British nose a bit higher in the air when she heard these remarks, and he saw tears squeeze out of the corners of her eyes. His father smiled grimly and joked back.

Niam hated him more than anything he had ever hated in his life.

The morning they were to leave, Will Scarlet himself came down to their breakfast fire. "Can I speak with your boy, John Weaver?"

Niam looked at his father just in time to catch the slight nod that was his only answer.

"Let's stretch our legs, lad," said Will, and they walked quietly beyond the camp for some minutes. The older man made a few comments about the weather and the poor hunting lately, remarks that needed no reply. Finally, they sat upon the bole of a great fallen tree. Will took out his knife and casually whittled at the stump of a branch.

"I suspect you're not happy to be leaving home, son," he said quietly. Niam had heard the man speak a thousand times, and it was always loudly, boastfully, bravely. Quiet talk from Will Scarlet he had never heard. "I remember when I first left home as a child, and when we all left home to come here. Both times made me angry."

Niam could think of nothing to reply, so he just nodded and pretended to watch a beetle exploring the forest floor.

"I wanted to give you a message—and ask a boon. The message is that if you find you can't stand the life where your family goes, we'll always take you back. We consider you one of the men."

Eyes filling quickly with tears, Niam looked into Scarlet's face. One of the men!

"Yes, lad. Robin says you're promising. And that's why we ask a boon."

"And what . . . ?" Niam couldn't finish.

"We want you to be our secret eyes and ears for a time. For at least two years, maybe longer. Wherever your folks end up, there will be king's business talked about. There will be roads and castles in the land of which we have no present knowledge. Learn what you can against the day one of us comes to ask for help. We might not have need of the help, ever, but that's how it is when you're a grown man. You have to prepare, whether or no. You have to be ready to protect your friends and family, even when nothing happens. Do you follow my meaning?"

Niam thought so, and nodded.

"That's the boon we ask. And let me add another thing. The

more successful you are, the more you'll be able to find out. You're a clever lad. You should study whatever you can. Think up some useful machines for the trades, maybe, like you did with that engine of yours. If you rise in the world, you'll be better able to help your old friends in the forest, and better able to help the poor."

Niam could see the sense in this. They were really asking him to stay away from the forest, though, and that was hard.

"I will do my best," he said.

It would have made Niam much happier to be leaving in the dark of night, to avoid embarrassment. But by the time the cart was actually loaded the jokes had stopped and folks were stopping by to say farewells. They brought cakes for the journey, small bags of dried venison, even a twelve-weight wheel of cheese. This was not the jeering departure Niam expected at all.

Three girls gave him locks of their hair for him to remember them by; two others wreaths of flowers, which he quickly hid inside his satchel.

Long after his father had put the traces over his shoulders and taken the cart's tongue poles in hand, folks were dropping by. A good dozen people walked with them the first four miles and right onto the Great North Road, laughing, singing, and trying not to talk about the separation. The Weavers were the first family, after all, to leave Sherwood and go back into the world again.

They were well on their way out of the forest when the friar caught up to them with his flea-bitten donkey struggling under the great weight. "Halloo, there, good John Weaver my son!" he shouted. "It's sacrilege to travel faster than the minister of the Lord. And unwise to depart without my blessing!"

Quickly he uttered a prayer in Latin, and then he took from his scrip a small purse. "This here is a hundred silver pennies, John Weaver, sent by Robin for your good use and to set you well upon the way. He understood that you were planning to go westward into Chester?"

"Aye, my wife has some people thereabouts," said John Weaver, holding the unexpected purse awkwardly. "If I can't find work, we might move on north, where the king's arm might not find us."

"Well, bear off on the west road at Blyth then. Robin has gone up to lift a few purses in Barnsdale, and some others are going Newark way to raise a fuss. There shouldn't be many sheriff's men along your road, not once the chase begins."

Then the friar put a hand on the cart pole and confidentially murmured something about good friends in Chester, and a letter being sent this morning by dispatch rider telling them to expect the Weavers by and by. "Just show this little piece of leather in the inn called the Sign of the Green Knight. You'll not want for a place in life."

Niam had never seen his father so touched. "Thank you, Brother," he said, almost stammering. "And thank him that sent you."

Hours later, with the last of the forest they knew disappearing behind them, and the Hathersage Pike Road that they did not know leading out before them, Niam took his turn in the cart harness. His father walked along just a step or so behind him. They had fallen in with a hide-monger's wagon train, well guarded, making its way west.

Niam was almost sick to his stomach with sadness, and finally he couldn't keep his tongue still anymore. "What was so wrong with what I did, Father? What was so wrong that we had to leave?"

Even before the words were out he expected a blow for his answer. He heard his mother's breath hiss in with surprise.

But no blow came. They went on for some time, with not a word. "It was just . . ." John Weaver began, and then the words stopped.

A few more steps. "It was just time to leave the forest, son. Long past time."

A few more steps. "I don't much care for man killing. I never have done. I don't much care for man-killing machines, neither."

And a few more steps. "But you did nothing wrong, Niam. Nothing. It was quite a thing you made. Quite a thing."

And a few more steps away from Sherwood Forest.

Then his father said something Niam had never expected to hear—in a low voice and ever so soft—but Niam heard it nonetheless.

"I was proud of you."

Herkens, god yemen,
Comley, corteys, and god,
On of the best that yever bare bowe,
Hes name was Roben Hode.

Harken, good yeomen,
Comely, courteous, and good,
One of the best that ever bore a bow,
His name was Robin Hood.

—from *Robin Hood and the Potter*

STRAIGHT AND TRUE

Robert J. Harris

The first thing you need to know about Robin Hood is that he wasn't really so expert an archer as many stories make him out to be. Will Scarlet was a better shot, and so was Little John on a good day. The thing with Robin was, he knew how *not* to shoot. What I mean is, once the arrow has flown, there you are standing defenseless while you reach for the next one. Robin knew better than any other how to keep the arrow nocked to the bow and menace several men at a time with it, holding them all at bay without actually loosing a single shaft. He could make every man among them feel that if he took a single step forward, he would be the one to receive an arrow through his heart.

The bishop of Knowlbridge had a similar gift. He could, in the course of a sermon, make mention of a certain sin, and at the same moment cast such a knowing eye over his congregation

Robin knew better than any other how to keep the arrow nocked to the bow . . .

that you had not the slightest doubt in your mind that he was referring to you in particular, even if you could not imagine how he had discerned your guilt. Many's the time I saw grown men break down and weep under the pressure of his imagined knowledge, then throw themselves at his feet to beg forgiveness.

It was hearing some of you young men grumbling about the conditions of your life—your talk of running off to the forest to become outlaws—that prompted me to speak to you like this in the first place. You think that all you need is a bow or a sword to improve your lot, but that is not so. It is the mind and the heart that are your greatest weapons, whether you be a farmer, an innkeeper or an outlaw. If you attend well to my story, you will see what I mean. It is a tale of Robin Hood that no one has heard before, for it was an exploit none of the rest of us witnessed and which he related to me alone.

To begin then. It was a heavy, sultry day in Sherwood, the sort of day when the deer really can't abide to be hunted and everyone sits around listlessly, gradually succumbing to a surly irritability. It was only a matter of time before Will Scarlet made an ill-considered remark to Little John, or Alan-a-Dale commenced one of those aggravating ditties that so set our teeth on edge. For all his skill on the lute, Alan was actually rather a poor singer, and most of his songs were of a satirical bent that was not to everyone's liking.

Marion's method of dealing with this sort of a day was to keep us all busy by chivvying us into tidying up the camp. She'd have us pick up the dead leaves and stuff them into sacks to make pillows or check the binding on the makeshift canopies that provided us with shelter or some other unnecessary exertion. I have never subscribed to the aphorism that the devil will find work for idle hands. It has been my long-held belief that too much bustle distracts the mind from thoughts of God, and that a carefree repose brings with it the very scent of the flowers of Eden. Marion, however, did not agree with my theology.

Robin saw the signs and gave me a dig in the ribs, rousing me from my noonday slumber. "Come on, Tuck," he said, "we need to get out of here."

Startled, I frantically rubbed my eyes and groaned, "What is it? The sheriff?"

"No, worse," Robin said. He inclined his head toward Marion, who was standing with her hands on her hips, frowning.

I crossed myself involuntarily. "Where shall we go?"

"It doesn't matter so long as we get there in a hurry."

He plucked up his bow and a quiver of arrows and slipped off silently into the trees. I followed with considerably less stealth, but, fortunately for me, Providence caused Much, the miller's son, to fall from his hiding place in a tree on the opposite side of the clearing. Marion immediately rushed to his side, first to aid him and then to assign him a host of domestic chores, which was the very thing he had been hiding from in the first place. While she was thus distracted, I successfully made my escape. Robin was waiting for me by the gnarled oak that was our usual meeting place on such occasions.

"Well, Robin, what say you we reconnoiter at the inn at Meadowsford?" I suggested, adjusting my habit. "I hear they have been brewing a fresh batch of their choice ale. It should have reached a pleasurable maturity by now."

"A worthy idea," Robin agreed, slapping me heartily on the back, "and if along the way we should happen upon an opportunity to separate a rich man from his wealth, so much the better."

Meadowsford was a pleasant cluster of thatched cottages overlooking a bubbling millstream. It took us two hours to get there, but no lesser distance would have put us entirely beyond the reach of Marion's organizational zeal. By the time we had seated ourselves at one of the tables outside the tavern and had attracted the attention of a serving wench, both my thirst and my hunger had been honed to a keen edge. When the new ale arrived, I enjoyed a few seconds of delicious anticipation before raising it to my lips. As I set the tankard down again with a glow of satisfaction, I could not help but notice that Robin's own ale lay untouched.

His eye had been caught by a trio of mounted figures who were trotting down the road in the direction of the forest. One was dressed in a fine mantle trimmed with fox fur and a pair of soft leather boots with parti-color lacing. The other two wore conical steel caps with nose guards that made them look absurdly like a pair of owls, and they carried heavy broadswords at their sides.

"From his garb, I would guess that fellow to be a merchant," Robin mused, "and a successful one at that."

"And from the look of the other two, I would surmise that he has hired himself some protection," I retorted. "Try the ale, Robin. It is everything its reputation proclaims it to be."

Robin was rubbing his chin thoughtfully. "There is an excellent spot for an ambush no more than a mile up that road," he recalled. "We could take a shortcut through the trees and be there ahead of them."

"No doubt we could," I said, "had we any desire to do so. Now, should we sample the pork or the mutton? Perhaps we could order a helping of each and share them?"

Robin rose to his feet and gathered up his weapons. The merchant and his escorts had now disappeared behind a copse of trees.

"Robin," I moaned, "we have only just arrived and I have scarcely had time to sip the foam from my ale."

"Stay here then, Tuck," he said. "I can handle this alone."

I shook my head as he departed, but I knew better than to try to dissuade him.

I never doubted that Robin would overtake his quarry. He sprinted through the forest with the easy speed of a true woodsman. Reflexes trained to avoid rabbit holes and tree roots, and a finely developed instinct for spotting the easiest path, allowed him to move through the dense woodland as swiftly as any other man could run along an open road.

He was scarcely even short of breath by the time he reached the site of his planned ambush, and he readied his bow. Soon he heard the clip-clop of hooves and the chatter of the approaching riders. When they were but a few yards away, Robin stepped out of hiding, planting himself directly in their path.

The merchant uttered a startled oath and reined in his horse, a sleek chestnut steed that was better fed than most of the villagers in the vicinity. Each of the men at arms automatically reached for his sword, but they both stopped short of drawing their blades. In spite of themselves they were daunted by Robin's ruthless expression and the quickness with which he raised his bow, shifting his aim nimbly from one of them to the other, thus threatening both at once.

"The first of you to draw a weapon will die before the blade clears the sheath," Robin promised them. "The second will have only one brief chance to strike me down before I fire my second arrow. If I were in your place, I would think carefully, for it is your very lives you are wagering."

The merchant glared angrily at his guards. "Are you in such fear of one lone man?" he demanded. "I brought you along to protect me against Bull Cutler and his entire band."

"But this is not Bull Cutler," one of the men at arms explained lamely. "This man is Robin Hood."

"Robin Hood?" the merchant repeated.

Robin made a small bow by way of acknowledgment.

Let me digress a moment. This incident took place not long after the archery contest where Robin had won the coveted silver arrow and snatched it out from under the nose of the Sheriff of Nottingham. Word had spread far and wide that Robin had split another man's arrow clean through to score the bull's-eye and take the prize. Now that tale, unlike some told of Robin Hood, is not entirely false, though it was vastly exaggerated. There had indeed been a contest for the silver arrow and in the end it came down to two bowmen, Robin and another fine shot, Gareth of Waycombe.

To settle the matter between them, the target was moved back to extreme range, so far indeed that some of the onlookers complained they could not see it. Gareth shot first, and he struck the target in the gold. However, due to the distance, the shaft did not fix well and drooped at an angle.

Now Robin knew that he had little chance of striking closer to the center, so he concentrated on putting as much pull on the bow as he could muster, letting the arrow fly with maximum force. He, too, struck the gold, but with an impact that jarred Gareth's arrow loose, causing it to fall to the ground. Since Robin's arrow had fixed and was the only one remaining on the target, he was declared the winner.

By the time we had eluded the sheriff's men—for the contest had been set up as a trap—and made our way back to Sherwood, the larger tale had already spread across the countryside: that Robin had split Gareth's arrow down the middle with his own shot, a feat I doubt could have been achieved by any bowman in England. Which clearly demonstrates that one of the greatest impulses to drive humankind is the need to embellish upon a story.

But back to my own tale, which I swear to you as a man of God, I have in no wise embellished or exaggerated. Although Robin's threat sprang as much from bravado as from his confidence in his own skill, nevertheless the merchant was also intimidated by the steely gleam in the outlaw's eye. With a grimace of frustration he pitched his purse at Robin's feet.

"I thank you for your cooperation," Robin told him with a grin, "and I urge you to be gone from these woods with all haste. Bull Cutler is indeed abroad in these parts, and he would take your life simply for the pleasure of doing harm, regardless of any profit to be had."

"I am fortunate then to have happened upon so civilized a brigand as yourself," the merchant said sarcastically, before spurring his horse forward.

He and his men continued on up the forest road and only when they were safely out of sight did Robin bend down to pick up the purse. He stuffed it into his belt and was about to make his way back to the tavern when four figures appeared suddenly from the trees, brandishing their weapons.

Robin knew at once it was Bull Cutler and his men. They were a bearded, unwashed crew whose vicious smiles exposed rows of yellowed and rotted teeth. The largest of them, armed with a curved sword, advanced on him: Bull Cutler himself.

"What have we here?" Cutler asked roughly. "Someone helping himself to loot that is ours by right. And letting a rich merchant leave with his life. That's something we can't allow, not even from you, Robin Hood."

He moved forward and his men with him.

Robin raised his bow menacingly. "A step closer," he warned, "and we shall see who is the first to die."

One or two of the robbers hesitated briefly as Robin swung

the point of his arrow from right to left and back again, pulling back on the bowstring as he did so. Their black-bearded chief, unfortunately, was not so easily intimidated.

Bull advanced with a determined stride, and Robin doubted that he would be distracted from his bloody course even if all his men were to fall dead around him. He tried pointing his arrow directly at Bull's heart, but the brigand continued to march forward unflinchingly. Bull was certainly well named, for he possessed either an unthinking courage or a bestial stupidity, which rendered him heedless of personal danger.

Robin considered the possibility that the other robbers might be demoralized if he killed their leader, giving him time to flee or at least fit another arrow to his bow and continue his retreat. Sometimes a band of men could be scattered by the slaying of their leader, but this course of action did not look hopeful.

For one thing, Bull was so massive that it might well take more than one shaft to bring him down. And even if one arrow were sufficient, the man to his left resembled him so closely, both in facial features as well as bulk, that he was unquestionably the bandit chief's scarcely less notorious brother, Ralph the Bear. There was every likelihood that the death of his brother would simply spur him forward in a frenzy of vengeance.

Robin knew without looking that he was still too far from the tree line to risk turning to flee. To do so would be to expose his back to a hurled dagger or ax, and one or two of the robbers looked like they might be swift enough to catch him before he could melt into the greenery.

It was then that a movement in the sky caught his eye. He

risked an upward glance and saw a dove fluttering about between the treetops. Above it, descending in a slow, confident spiral, was a hawk, closing on its prey with outstretched talons, waiting for the perfect moment to drop and claim its prize.

"You all look to me like men who are not afraid of a wager," Robin said suddenly. "Would you match your reputation with mine, Bull Cutler, to see which of us is the better man?"

Bull's eyes narrowed suspiciously. "Are these to be your last words?" he asked contemptuously.

"See above us." Robin pointed his arrow upward. "There is a killing about to take place."

Bull's eyes darted up for a fraction of a second then fixed their murderous gaze back on Robin. "That makes two," he growled.

"I'll wager that I can shoot just as the hawk strikes, skewering both birds with one arrow," Robin said with all the arrogance he could muster.

"No man can make such a shot," Bull scoffed.

"They say he's good," Bear pointed out.

"I'd like to see him try," one of the other men chimed in. "It would be a tale to tell."

Robin could tell that the notion had made a suitable impression on the brigands and that Bull was considering it.

"If I make the shot," Robin said, "do you swear that you will let me live?"

"Go on, Bull," the leader's brother urged him. "Let's see him try it."

A sneer curled Bull's lip and he nodded. "Go ahead, bowman. Win your life, if you can." He made very little attempt to sound sincere and Robin did not suppose for a moment that he would keep his word.

The brigands gave Robin coarse and derisive encouragement as he licked his lips and raised his bow dramatically, fixing his eyes on the hawk. The merciless hunter was descending in an elegant series of narrowing circles, its wings fully spread, its gaze concentrated upon its unsuspecting prey. The robbers looked up also, but Robin could see from the corner of his eye that Bull was still half watching him.

Drawing his arm back and exerting the maximum pull on the bow, Robin held his position, his eyes sharply following the movements of the two birds. His muscles were beginning to ache with the tension when the hawk suddenly folded its wings and dropped toward its target with the speed of a falling stone, its sharp claws extended. At that crucial instant Robin released the bowstring.

The arrow shot straight up, and the eyes of every one of the brigands, Bull included, followed its flight with hushed expectancy. The arrowhead stabbed right into the hawk's breast and it fell away to one side before plummeting toward the ground below. The dove flew off in a startled flutter of wings, leaving behind a few stray feathers that had been snatched loose by the hawk's claws the instant the arrow had hit home.

Bull let out a scornful laugh and turned a contemptuous face toward Robin.

But Robin, of course, was gone.

The brief moment the bandits had spent watching the flight of the arrow and the dove's escape had been all he needed to turn and plunge silently into the thick of the forest where he could easily outdistance them. Bull and his men charged into the woodland, hacking at the foliage with their weapons and cursing Robin Hood for his trickery, but it availed them nothing.

When Robin rejoined me at the tavern, I had already disposed of a helping of succulent pork and was setting about a joint of beef with all the enthusiasm its aroma merited. So great was his relief at his escape that he downed a tankard of ale in one quaff and told me the whole story in very much the same words I have just told it to you.

Could Robin have made the shot if he had wished to, you ask?

That is hardly the point. If he had, he would have caused two deaths. By missing he saved two lives, his own and that of the dove. So did he shoot straight and true? Debate that among yourselves if you must, but do not keep a hungry storyteller from his reward. Was there not some mention made of venison?

And if you would be doubly blessed, then pass me that tankard of ale.

. . . come and dwell with me?
And twice in a yeere thy clothing be changed
If my man thou wilt bee,
The tone shall be of light Lincolne greene,
And tother of Picklory.

. . . come and live with me?
And twice a year your clothing will be changed,
If my man you will be,
The one the color of light Lincoln green,
The other of Picklory.

—from *Robin Hood and
the Pinder of Wakefield*

At Fountain Abbey

Mary Frances Zambreno

Late spring—rain lashed against the gathering dawn as Gib struggled through the underbrush. Branches caught at his clothing, slashing his face and hands as he fought his way through. Far above, clouds scudded across the sky like living things driven by the chill wind. He paused, breathing heavily and wishing for surer footing—or even for a horse. But the main road was dangerous, with the hunt up for him, and he hadn't dared try for a horse. No time—he'd fled on foot, from almost the moment of his mother's death.

Two days—two days and almost two nights, he'd been living wild, scrounging for food where he could find it and sleeping in snatches on the cold, damp earth. Eyes fixed on the rough ground, he almost banged his nose on the little paling—the sort kept around a byre. Cows, sheep—aha, chickens! A stone bulk loomed over the dark treetops, outlined by the stars. Fountain Abbey. At last.

"Go to the abbey," his mother had told him, with almost her dying breath. *"Go to Sherwood Forest. You will be safe there . . ."*

"My father—my father was a forester," she'd whispered, pulling him close with all of her fading strength. A pretty woman, the fever had left her wasted, her skin like yellow parchment stretching over bone.

"What do you mean?" he'd asked, puzzled, blinking back tears. "Your father was the Earl of Huntingdon."

"No! No," she'd insisted, shaking her head back and forth against the pillow. "That was . . . the story we gave out. After." Hollow eyes flickered sideways, to where his uncle's chaplain waited by the window, driven off only briefly by a son's right to say a private farewell. "He was a forester in Sherwood . . ." A spasm of coughing shook her, and she gasped for breath, her fingers digging clawlike into his arm.

"It doesn't matter," he'd said, alarmed. "Rest now. In the morning—"

"No more mornings," she said painfully. "No time. I should have told you—before. *Your* father knew . . . the truth. I'd not have married him, else. But your uncle . . . Lord Richard means you harm."

"Well, I know that." That his father's brother wanted him out of the way in order to inherit his father's estate was scarcely news; for most of his thirteen years, Gib had lived in the shadow of his uncle's malice. "But—"

She ignored the interruption. "Gib—my Gilbert—I pray you—go to Sherwood. To the brothers at Fountain Abbey. You will be safe from your uncle . . . in the old forest."

She collapsed backward, then, coughing. Desperately, he had called for the physician, for anyone to come and help—but it was too late. The Lady Hermione had died without speaking another word.

Why Sherwood? Gib wondered even now, remembering. Once upon a time he'd loved sitting by the fire to listen to the old songs and tales—dreamed of roaming through the forest like Robin Hood—but this was real life, not a song. *It makes no sense.*

They had cost her, those last words, and for the life of him, he hadn't a clue what she had meant. Saintly though the brothers of Fountain Abbey might be, no unworldly community of holy men could stand for long against Baron Richard Glentham of Brinsdale. The most Gib could hope for at the abbey was a chance to rest, and perhaps a horse or an escort to help him reach the king. His Majesty had little liking for the growing arrogance of his northern barons; he'd be most displeased to hear that Lord Richard Glentham meant to make himself more powerful by adding to his own those lands that should belong to his brother's son . . .

Well. He was here, now. Carefully, he skirted the little byre, avoiding the sleepy chickens roosting in the eaves—it didn't look big enough to stable horses; perhaps he'd have to be content with borrowing the abbot's mule. The gray light was growing stronger; everything held motionless, waiting for day. Some-

Why Sherwood? Gib wondered.

where, the brothers were chanting the morning office—he could just hear the rise and fall of their voices, as if from a great distance.

He was crossing the grounds, looking for the guesthouse, when he saw the abbey chapel: a squat stone building with narrow windows high on the walls—they looked more like arrow slits than church windows—and marked by a simple stone cross. Only the one great door set deep into the west wall, by the look of things. It was like any of a thousand churches, smaller than some, and older, but there was something about it that made him pause. *It looks—familiar,* he thought. *Like something in a dream . . .*

Noise—metal on leather, a familiar creaking—he whirled, cursing his distraction, but it was too late. Closing in on him was a company of his uncle's men, mounted and foot both.

A trap! Instinctively, Gib lashed out, but the nearest man caught at his arm, twisting it behind his back. *They were ahead of me.*

"Well, nephew," said Lord Richard Glentham, leaning over the neck of his black warhorse. Gib stared up into the familiar, sharp-featured face, the cold gray eyes under arched brows. "You've led us a merry chase. Make sure of him." He nodded at the man holding Gib, who raised a mailed fist—

The back of his head exploded with pain, and the world went dark.

He woke slowly, lapped in warmth. There was something soft beneath his head, and his nose tickled. For a moment, his mind resisted, seeking the comfort of unconsciousness—and then he sneezed, and his eyes blinked open.

103

"Awake, are you?" said his uncle. Lord Richard was sitting at his ease, leaning back in a leather-padded chair with a tankard of ale in one hand. His lips quirked sardonically. "About time. Tammas hit you a little too hard, it seems."

Gib tensed, trying to get his feet under him, but his hands were tied roughly behind his back—no chance. Yet. His head ached.

"What I do not understand, my lord, is how you tracked him to Fountain Abbey," said another man, who was wearing the brown habit of a Franciscan friar. He was an old man, the shaven tonsure of his round head scarcely necessary now, since his hair was only a few wisps of fluffy white over his ears. The coarse cloth of his robe fell in shrunken folds over what must once have been a prodigious paunch: it was said that the abbot of Fountain Abbey had been a great trencherman—a tremendous eater—in his youth. "Surely, most runaways would head for London, and not for old Sherwood."

Lord Richard snorted. "Not this one. The boy is Robin Hood mad, forever seeking out some minstrel or other to listen to the old ballads. The moment we discovered he'd escaped—that is, that he was missing—I knew he'd head for the forest."

Gib withered at the scorn in his uncle's voice. He *did* know better than to seek safety in Sherwood, songs or no. But he would not give Lord Richard the satisfaction of hearing him try to explain that he'd been fulfilling his mother's final request.

"Tsk." The abbot shook his head. "It's certain, then, that he isn't your brother's son?"

"Certain." Richard took a pull from his tankard. "According

to my sister-in-law's deathbed confession, he's the brat of some wandering musician or other. Explains the way she always dithered over the minstrels, I suppose, filling the boy's head with moonshine and ballads. Blood will tell, no doubt."

"No doubt," said the abbot, nodding solemn agreement.

"You lie!" Gib burst out, unable to hold back. Whatever Lady Hermione had meant with her last words, it had not been *that*.

Lord Richard grinned sardonically. "You see, Abbot? How steeped in sin he is? Perhaps he hoped for a miracle—for Robin Hood and all his merry band to return, as if by magic, just so that he might join them."

"Indeed, my lord, he should have known better," the abbot said sadly. "Poor, foolish boy, Robin o' the Greenwood has been dead since before you were born. If he were alive today, he would be an old, old man—as old as I am, perhaps. There are no such miracles left in the world . . ." Gib looked away, unable to meet his gaze.

There was a noise at the door, and the abbot held up one hand. "Enter."

A brother with bright blue eyes and the nut-brown face of a man who had worked much out of doors came in. "You sent for me, Father Abbot?"

"Brother Mitchell, of course. Excuse the interruption, my lord—"

Lord Richard nodded gracious permission. Tankard in hand, he walked over to the hearth and looked down at Gib. "Well, boy, it seems I've won at last," he said, low-voiced.

"You lie," Gib said, equally low-voiced. "You *know* you lie."

"Do I?" his uncle said, lip curling. "I have your mother's signed confession in writing, all properly witnessed by my chaplain—more than enough for the manor court."

His court, he meant, under his control. "Take the lands, then, if they mean so much to you," Gib said desperately, knowing the plea was useless even as he spoke. "Just let me go. I'll swear any oath you want."

"And leave you free to carry your tale of woe to the king? No, brat, I will not. Content yourself with being my guest—for as long as you live." Gib flinched at the menace in his tone, and the baron smiled. "You should never have run to Sherwood, nephew. It was easy to outflank you."

The abbot came up beside them. "My lord, Brother Mitchell informs me that the table is set. You will dine with us?"

Lord Richard hesitated, and Gib caught his breath: the abbot's table was famous. *Please, Blessed Mary, let him stay to dine. All I need is a chance.* "Why, I'd planned to be back in Brinsdale by sunset," his uncle said slowly.

"So you shall, so you shall. It's early yet, and the days are growing longer toward summer," the abbot said briskly. "I've a venison pasty it would be churlish not to share."

"Very well." Lord Richard drained his tankard decisively. "Since you offer so graciously, I'll dine with you, Abbot. But, by your leave, I'll have a word with my men first."

"Of course, of course," the abbot said, chivvying him along. "Not but what the boy isn't secure enough, with your guards all around the abbey."

The door closed behind them, leaving Gib alone. *Thank you,*

Blessed Mary. Writhing, he twisted his body, stretching at the shoulders: arms under hips, wrists to knees—a wrench that left him gasping, and his hands were in front of him. Instantly he started to chew the leather thong, strong young teeth biting into the knot. It was new leather, nearly raw—it gave when he pulled and twisted. There!

The window was locked, but from the inside only, and the ground wasn't too far for someone limber and desperate to make a leap for it. His feet were under him, ready to spring—and then he heard movement at the door.

"I'll just fetch the abbot's wooden spoon," said the cheerful voice of Brother Mitchell. "He won't be comfortable eating without it. Our order forbids silver, you know, though of course we keep it for guests."

He came through the door, blue eyes widening as he took in Gib's posture. "What—"

Gib leaped, pushing Brother Mitchell forward in his rush, overbalancing the man into one of the two guards on either side of the open door.

"Heyla!" the guard cried, going over backward with the brother on top of him.

"Look out!" said the one still standing, raising a crossbow. Gib ducked as the bolt clattered over his head.

"Don't shoot!" Brother Mitchell said, reaching up from the floor.

"Let go my arm, Brother," the man snarled. "If we lose him, Lord Richard will have our heads in place of his!"

Gib had no time to wonder at Brother Mitchell's mercy—he

was away, off down the long cloister with feet pounding behind him. Smells of food and cooking—the refectory, a brief glimpse of the abbot's startled face, his uncle's angry one, the long table full of brothers. He bent, ducking under the trestle, sending a server sprawling in a clatter of cutlery.

"Get him!" Lord Richard roared. "There, by the entryway!"

The kitchen, with the fat cook bending over the hearth and a novice turning the spit—savory odors made his mouth water, even in his haste. A fat orange and white tomcat basked in a patch of sun by the door.

"Sorry," he told the beast, and bent to scoop him up in both arms. The cat hissed, and Gib avoided claws just long enough to hurl the animal back through the door and full into the face of the first guardsmen coming through it.

"Yiee!" the man yelled, as the cat squalled in protest of such treatment. The guard fell backward, blocking the way. Grinning at the astounded cook, Gib saluted, and dashed into the abbey grounds. Lord Richard's men were grouped by the fountain, dicing. Ten—twenty—he hadn't known there would be so many! He spun on his heel in the opposite direction. They were too close—he wasn't going to make it. He ducked under an outstretched arm of one, hurdling the water trough.

Right—left—around another corner—and then he saw the open door of the abbey chapel, cool and dark. A moment's hesitation and he was inside, the door clanging shut behind him. Breathing heavily, he waited for an instant while his eyes adjusted to the dimness. There should be—yes! He wrestled the heavy crossbar into place inside the door, latching it closed just as the first blow thudded home against the outside.

Silence. Men yelling in anger—sound of steel against wood. The door juddered, but held firm. He was safe—for the moment.

Idiot! he scolded himself, eyes sweeping the interior of the chapel. There had to be another way out—but there wasn't. *What were you thinking?* In his haste, he'd trapped himself. Unless the abbot . . .

He pressed his ear against the door, and listened, heart beating fast.

"Break it down!" the baron raved. "Break down the door!"

"My lord, this is a house of God!" the abbot said, shocked. It was as he'd hoped: the abbot protested, and even his uncle's hardest men wouldn't relish the thought of profaning a church. "You would not!"

"I don't care if it's St. Peter's in Rome," Lord Richard shouted. "You, Tammas, Abel—do as I say! Break down this door!"

A whispered conversation; the men were uneasy, and Gib strained to hear. The abbot twittered another protest. "My lord, give it time. I'm sure the boy will think better of his defiance in a few hours. We will pray that he see reason, my brothers and I. He has no food or water . . ."

Well, that's true enough, Gib thought. His stomach rumbled, and he thought wistfully of the rich food in the abbey kitchen. At least there had been plenty of rain yesterday, so he wasn't particularly thirsty.

He could almost hear his uncle thinking it through. And thinking that no man seeking power should risk outraging the church.

"Dawn," the baron said finally, curtly. "I'll give you until dawn to pray, Abbot. If he isn't out by then, we'll break down the door. In the meanwhile, I want this place guarded so that not even a mouse could slip past."

There was a relieved murmur from his men. Gib closed his eyes, and breathed a brief prayer of thanks. Until dawn, he still had a chance.

Turning, he inspected his new prison. The little chapel was clean and swept, with more than enough light filtering through the thick bubbled glass of narrow windows to see by. The altar had a statue of the Virgin, old and worn but touched up with bright blue paint; a small vase of pink wild roses sat in front of it. Candle sconces were set in rough niches along the walls, ready for evening prayers.

The windows were the only possible escape route. As soon as he'd caught his breath, Gib shinnied up one rough stone wall to check: he thought he could squeeze through a window, given time, but his uncle's men had made camp in a great perimeter circle all around the chapel. They were piling mounds of firewood on each of the four sides, so that firelight would illuminate the entire building by night.

Discouraged, he jumped back to the floor. *I'll have to wait for darkness,* he thought. *Break a window and try to slip past.* But in his heart, he knew it wouldn't work. He'd be taken again, and this time his uncle would not be so careless. *Blessed Mary, you helped me once. What should I do now?*

Exhausted, he huddled against the great wooden door, and dozed.

A man knelt in prayer in front of the altar. For a moment, Gib thought that one of the brothers had slipped in somehow, but then he saw that the man was wearing no habit but a leather jerkin and leggings, with soft boots laced up to the knee. He stared, puzzled, at the back of the fair head bent so devoutly. The man crossed himself, stood up, and turned—and blue eyes like the summer sky met Gib's. He grinned so infectiously that even in his confusion Gib couldn't help but smile back, and then the man beckoned to him, pointing at the altar . . .

Gib woke with a start. He was alone in the chapel. By the fading light streaming through the windows, it was sunset.

What a peculiar dream, he thought. Outside, he could hear the noise of guards settling down to watch for the night. *A man praying—did he mean I should pray, too?* Dreams could be meaningful, he knew, but their meaning was often difficult to decipher. *No, he was pointing at something.*

Thoughtfully, Gib inspected the altar. It was a perfectly ordinary stone rectangle, a bit rough-edged at the back. When he felt around behind it, he realized that there was more space than he'd thought back there: a few moments struggling and straining revealed a square of wood set into the floor against the base

111

of the altar. His fingers traced an inscription—Matt. 7:7. Matthew, chapter seven, verse seven: *Ask, and it shall be given you; knock, and it shall be opened* . . .

Frowning, he sat on his heels. Then, shrugging, he leaned forward to knock sharply in the center of the wooden square.

"Oh!" There was a rush of cold air, and the floor gave way underneath him. He fell, banging his head painfully.

When his eyes adjusted, he saw that he was in a cellar. There was a ladder behind him, fastened to the wall with long nails; next to it on a little shelf was the stub of a candle, with flint and tinder ready to hand. But that wasn't important. He sniffed: fresh air! Hardly daring to hope, he fumbled for the flint, lit the little candle and held it high.

The strange place was about half the size of the chapel above, and built later, to judge by the way the foundation came only halfway down. The walls were crude, set inexpertly with uneven stones along the base, and the floor was dirt. It was empty, except for a long, low chest built of rough-hewn planks; the lid was ill fitting.

On the back wall was a tunnel, dark and earthy but carefully shored up with what looked like fresh timbers. He stared at it, trembling. A way out . . . but why did the brothers need a hidden tunnel under their chapel? Unless they had something to hide.

He walked over to the chest and lifted the lid. What he saw there made him gasp: a glitter of gold and silver reflected the candlelight. There were lengths of soft velvet, and figured silk, a tapestry folded carefully in one corner. From the mouth of one small bag spilled brilliant gems—rubies, emeralds, sapphires. Why, the wealth of the Indies was here! A king's ransom . . .

Then he saw it—inside the lid of the chest, carefully fastened on hooks as if it were a precious relic, was a longbow shaped out of fine yew. Arrows fletched with gray goose feathers filled the old quiver beside it, and next to that a cloth hat with a feather in it—a hat cut of the rich forest green material dyed only in Lincoln.

A king's ransom—or an outlaw's. A gray goose shaft and a hat of Lincoln green: This was Fountain Abbey, in old Sherwood. *But why all the gold and silver, here in the abbey? Oh, of course!* Of course Robin Hood would have stored some portion of gathered riches, to be kept against future need. When he died, his men would have hidden the remaining treasure safely away—with other precious things. Wonderingly, reverently, Gib touched the bow. He'd no skill in the longbow. It was a yeoman's weapon, not a nobleman's. A forester's . . .

He could leave now. Wherever the little tunnel led, it was surely beyond the perimeter guard. He could be five miles off by dawn, and, yes, with enough gold to buy his own way anywhere in the world, if he wished. But then, in the morning, his uncle would beat down the chapel door to find him gone.

He's no fool, Gib realized, with gathering dismay. *If I'm not seen to leave, he'll assume I must be hiding somewhere in the chapel, and he'll take the building apart, stone by stone, looking for my hiding place. The brothers won't be able to stop him. He'll find the tunnel and the treasure and all. He'll say that the brothers must have had dealings outside the law, and he'll condemn them to death or prison for their crimes—and then he'll take the treasure for his own. It isn't fair, it isn't right, but he'll do it, and the abbey will be destroyed. Unless I am* seen *to leave . . .*

Hastily, he began to rummage through the chest. He couldn't use the longbow, but surely there was something . . . ah. A wide belt, of soft leather—with strings pulled from one of the pouches, it made a fair sling. Not a nobleman's weapon, either, but a boy's, and he was better at it than most. He'd a good eye, his arms master had always said. He'd need to search out pebbles—no. Alight with mischief, he scooped up a handful of gold coins. They'd do, and if anyone found them, it would only be another distraction for the guards.

Makeshift sling in hand, he headed for the tunnel. No time to waste—he had a suspicion that the abbot meant to get him out before dawn somehow. Probably the man had some plan of his own, if the abbot was who Gib now suspected he was, but Gib couldn't risk the wait. *Wonder if he sends Brother Mitchell?* He rather thought he might know Brother Mitchell from the ballads, too. *Not Will Scathelock or Alan the Minstrel, no. They'd be Robin's own age, and not so much younger than—than the abbot. But the miller's boy . . . it could be him.*

Firmly, he put speculation aside. He had work to do.

Dawn again, crouching in the underbrush. He'd come full circle in twenty-four hours, but he knew where he was now, and what he was going to do. He squinted at the chapel—there was just enough light to touch the east windows. Stealthily, he edged sideways, aiming for a clear shot. Settling one of the heavy coins into the leather strap of his sling, he whirled—released.

Crash! Direct hit. The glass broke, with a shuddering cascade. It fell inside the chapel, but he'd just have to hope that no one noticed. Another coin—another window—on the north wall, this time.

"He's trying to escape!" A guardsman shouted.

"Where?"

"There, you fool, by the window! Wake the baron!"

Gib grinned, slipped around to the left by the picketed horses—they were restive, whinnying at the noise. The guards were milling around the chapel; when he made his move, they'd think he'd gotten past them in the dark. Then all he had to do was keep them stirred up enough to follow him without asking *how* he'd gotten past them . . .

Another coin, and the west wall lost a window.

"He's on this side!"

More confusion. Shoving the sling into the front of his tunic, Gib ducked under the picket line, unsettling the horses still further. They stamped and reared back, discovering that their hobbles were loose and that the pickets had been untied—all but one. Swinging himself on the back of his uncle's black stallion, he pointed the beast at the open area in front of the chapel, kicked his heels into its sides, and shouted.

"Run! Run, you black devil!"

The stallion screamed, leaping forward in its anger. Gib bent over the neck, gripping the coarse mane. He had a quick glimpse of his uncle on the steps of the abbey guesthouse, face engorged with fury.

"My warhorse! After him!"

Gib risked a mocking wave, laughing with sheer exuberance. Then he and the horse were away, pounding into the forest path while behind him the sounds of pursuit gathered. He counted: one turn—two—three turns. Time enough for those who had managed to catch a horse to be after him. The stallion hurdled a fallen log and Gib hung on grimly. They splashed along a streambed, startling a heron—four, five, six turns. Time enough so even the men on foot ought to have joined in the chase. He glanced back over his shoulder—yes, there were the mounted guards. Only three, but they were just close enough to lead the rest astray. Yanking the stallion's head sideways, he spun around the seventh turn—

—and caught at a low-hanging branch with both hands, swinging himself up into the tree. The stallion didn't even pause. Gib settled himself into the leaves as the guardsmen thundered past—and then more guards—then his uncle, shouting in anger—and finally the pikemen, struggling along on foot. He'd found this place the night before, by moonlight; the branch was low enough to reach but easy to hang on to, and there was plenty of cover.

He waited, while the sounds of pursuit vanished into the forest—until the sun was high in the sky and he was sure that his uncle would not come back. Then he leaped to the ground, landing lightly.

Safe. And he had been seen to leave, so the abbey was safe, too.

The sensible thing to do now would be to head for London, for the king. The sensible thing . . .

He turned, and started walking slowly back toward Fountain Abbey.

When he arrived, they were waiting for him. The abbot and Brother Mitchell and others whose names he did not know gathered in a small, quiet group in front of the chapel.

"You came back," said the abbot—who had once been known as Friar Tuck. "I thought you might."

Gib swallowed. "I did." *Now what?*

"I believe that these belong to you," the abbot said, holding out the longbow and the quiver of arrows. "Your grandfather would have wanted you to have them."

"My grandfather—my grandfather was a forester," Gib said stupidly, feeling the weight of the unfamiliar weapon in his hands. "My mother told me, when she died. And then she didn't have time . . ."

Tuck nodded somberly. "Probably she never dared to speak of it before then, poor girl, and she the last of the line. It's true enough, so far as it goes. Your grandfather was a forester—but he was something more than a forester as well, in his day. Something that's still needed, perhaps, with the king far away in London town and men like the baron running the world. A boy who could find out our secrets and yet not betray us might well understand the need for that something. Or someone."

Gib caressed the curved wood of the bow, trying to make sense of the abbot's words and thinking how smooth the grain of the yew felt against his palms—how strangely familiar. Remembering . . . his mother's face, when she spoke of her father, in those last few painful breaths . . . his uncle's greed, fueled by the hunger for power . . . and the treasure in the chapel, kept safe from men like Lord Richard for who knew how many years. Waiting.

Above all, he remembered the man in his dream, who had turned and smiled at him, beckoning him forward.

His grandfather. Robin Hood.

"But—but I don't know the forest," he protested. "Not really. I've never even held a longbow before!"

There was relieved laughter at that, and the abbot's face relaxed into a broad smile.

"That's all right, lad," said Much, the miller's son—now called Brother Mitchell. "We'll teach you."

Lyth and lysten, gentil men,
And herken what I shall say.
How the proude sheryfe of Notyngham
Dyde crye a full fayre play;

That all the best archers of the north
Sholde come upon a day,
And he that shoteth allther best
The game shall bere a way.

Give ear and listen, gentlemen,
And hark to what I shall say.
How the proud Sheriff of Nottingham
Did proclaim a full fair game;

That all the best archers of the north
Should come upon a day,
And he who shot the best of all
Would bear the prize away.

      —from *A Gest of Robyn Hode,*
         fytte five. (281–3)

Robin Hood v. 1.5.3

Adam Stemple

The tall, gray gates to the institute swung slowly open and a large gray car drove through them at a sedate pace. When it reached the front door, the car door was opened and held for a small gray man who carried a small gray briefcase. Ignoring the offer of help from the chauffeur, the polite nod of the doorman, the frowns of the security guards at the metal detector, the "what floor?" of the elevator operator, and the downright panicked cries of three receptionists, he marched straight into an office marked *Private: Do Not Enter.*

"Who was in charge until I arrived?"

The small man spoke with a nasal twang. His chin quivered slightly as he spoke and a black goatee tried in vain to cover the motion. He looked the small office over and decided to visit his wrath upon the sole resident. This unsuspecting soul was just finishing a bowl of soup and jumped to his feet, spilling the remnants down his front. Judging from the state of his pants and chair, it was not the first time. He didn't look as if he should be a nervous man, however; he was tall, blond, and attractive in an assistant hockey coach kind of way.

"I am. Was. Were," the blond man stuttered. "Gibson at your service, sir. You must be . . . uh . . . Mr. Marschall?" He wiped his hand off on his pitiful trousers and offered it to the smaller man, who eyed it as if it were a small muddy dog that had just relieved itself on the front seat of his mother's sedan.

"Brief me."

Mr. Marschall settled into the chair Gibson had vacated and, even from this less elevated position, managed to look down his not inconsiderable nose at the taller man.

"Well, sir," Gibson said, and coughed nervously. "You know about ASIF?"

"Allied Systems International Financier. Built in 2007 to control the economy of the EEC, OAS, and such countries that wished everlasting financial security; the new breed of AI, self-aware, self learning, etc. Go on."

"It's gone mad."

Marschall pulled on his mustache and raised one eyebrow.

"Mad?"

"It's redistributing the wealth of the world in shocking new ways, sir."

"Redistributing how?"

"It seems to be systematically removing the capital assets of the larger, well-established, and affluent companies and giving them to underdeveloped countries and welfare organizations."

"Start at the beginning," Marschall told the taller man, and shifted in the chair to avoid a puddle that he hoped was only soup.

"It all started two weeks ago during the madness of the government downsizings. It seems Dick King was accidentally canned."

"The CEO's brother?"

"Yes, he was also ASIF's original programmer. During a talk with the First Lady, the CEO apparently said, and I quote here"—Gibson leaned over Marschall, muttered a sheepish "excuse me," and rummaged through some loose papers on his desk until he came up with a gum wrapper—"Here it is." He squinted at the tiny print on the wrapper and read, " 'I wish someone would rid me of my pain-in-the-ass brother. He's becoming a real nuisance.' " He put the wrapper down after a brief yet thorough investigation of it, perhaps looking for any leftover gum, and went on. "An eavesdropping, overzealous staff member decided to show initiative."

Mr. Marschall shook his head and clucked his tongue on his palate, intimating his disapproval of this individual in particular and initiative in general.

"The overzealous staff member was let go himself in the downsizing, so news of the CEO's brother's departure didn't reach him until the damage had already been done. Like most programmers, Dick King was quite eccentric and not exactly trustworthy." The blond man shot a worried glance at Marschall before going on bravely. "But the CEO had always been able to keep him under control before. When he was fired, however, he snapped. The revenge he exacted was bizarre."

"Well," said Marschall. "Why can't we just rehire Mr. King, explain the facts, apologize, and have him repair the damage he's done? Or rehire him, forget the explanation, and use torture or drugs or a combination of both to convince him to repair the damage, whatever it is?"

"I'm afraid we can't rehire him, sir."

"Why not?"

"A young, motivated CIA operative overheard the conversation as well."

"Ah." Marschall grumbled. "Mr. King is dead then?"

"We believe he is at the bottom of the Potomac. And Chesapeake Bay." Gibson looked uncomfortable. "And the Lincoln Memorial."

Marschall examined his fingernails for a moment then asked, "And this revenge, it involves ASIF?"

"I think you'd better see for yourself, sir."

Marschall left his chair and followed Gibson out the door, down the single hallway, through three doors, past four visible security checkpoints, two invisible ones, and a potential full-cavity search until they reached a door marked: ASIF Command Center—Authorized Personnel Only.

Gibson started to warn his new boss of the oddities that lay behind the door, but the smaller man rushed past him before the warning could be delivered. As Marschall went through the door he was brought up short by a robust voice crying, "Hold!"

"Eep?" Marschall seemed to say.

"Hold! Stand where thou art. For I say thou art a fat pigeon who must needs be plucked of his purse! Or mayhaps thee would prefer it if I plucked my bowstrings and let fly a goose-feather shaft through thy breast?" A robust laugh filled the room, and yet the room itself was empty except for an office chair, a phone, two paintings of rural scenes, and a computer that was surprisingly small considering it controlled most of the civilized world's finances.

Marschall recovered himself quickly and sat in the chair. "ASIF," he said authoritatively to the computer, "recognize Marschall, password." Here he typed in something and touched his mustache self-consciously.

The computer replied instantly. "I recognize thee, Sheriff! Prithee, how could I not, thou black dog? It did not take the Usurper long to hire thee."

In what seemed like one smooth motion, Marschall put his briefcase on the desk, opened it, took a disk out of it, and slid it into the computer. Smiling inwardly, he said, "ASIF, run program Cleanser 3.7."

The disk drive whirred, and the sound of clashing swords came pouring from the computer's speakers. "Thou wouldst murder me, wouldst thou? By my faith, look to thyself, fellow!"

There was a small ringing and Marschall unhooked a mini-cellular from his belt. He answered and his face showed color for the first time.

"No, I did not authorize a ten thousand dollar purchase," he stated to the caller; and then to the computer, "ASIF, run program Deletex 2.3.1."

"Ha! Thou wished to take my life and yet thou take it mightily hard when I take thy gold. I will have thy ill-gotten gains from thee, even though I hang for it as high e'er a forest tree in Sherwood!"

The programs Viroid 1.3, Remover 5.0.1, and the Beta version of something called *Kill!Kill!* seemed to have no effect, and the disk ejected itself from the computer as Marschall pulled a cord out of the back of his briefcase and plugged it directly into the computer. He flipped back a leather false bottom and began tapping on the keyboard beneath it.

"Thou art no match for me, Sheriff! I could defeat thee with a gigabyte tied behind my back," cried the computer. "Nay, two! Wouldst thou meet on the field of battle? Ha! There goes thy house! Thy car! Thy credit!"

Marschall bit his lower lip and pulled a trackball out of his jacket pocket. He plugged it into his briefcase and spun it, hitting the various buttons in a vaguely Caribbean rhythm.

"Here is merry sport afoot! A numbered Swiss bank account!"

Chuckling erupted from the computer's speakers and Marschall blanched. With shaking hands he pulled a full Virtual Reality rig out of his seemingly bottomless briefcase and strapped on the helmet and gloves.

Over the next two hours, Marschall lost three savings accounts, two checking accounts, four credit cards, the Swiss bank account, his house, two cars, and had somehow accrued a gambling debt that would most likely get him killed by the mob inside of a month. After he lost the last of his tax-sheltered annuities, he angrily stripped off his VR rig and picked up the office chair.

"How about a little of this, you insane excuse for an overrated calculator?" he screamed, beating the small computer with the chair.

The computer answered, "Insane? Is it madness to provide for the penniless?" The chair slammed down on the monitor, sending up a shower of sparks. "To feed the famished or house the homeless?"

Again the chair came down, and this time the space bar flew from the keyboard, hitting Marschall in the chest. The computer's voice rose in pitch and the speakers popped and crackled. "To desire dignity for both Saxon and Norman alike?" the computer cried.

A third time the chair descended, and the voice fell silent. When Gibson and three security guards finally pulled the enraged little man away, there was nothing left of either the chair or ASIF. Marschall's face was flushed and his breathing came short and irregular.

"I'll need to file an extra expense account for this job," he said to no one in particular.

His phone rang. He answered warily, and a now-familiar voice issued from it.

"Thou art no match for Robin Hood! There are more hiding places on the Internet than in the entire forest of Sherwood. I shall continue to steal from the rich and give to the poor until

"Thou art no match for Robin Hood!"

Good King Richard returns to the throne. Death to all usurpers! By the way, this call cost thee thirty thousand dollars."

Marschall sat heavily on the floor with the phone buzzing softly in his hand. Gibson looked concerned, and the three guards looked confused. Eventually, the guards lost interest and wandered off. The spectacle of a grown man—or semi-grown in Marschall's case—sitting on the floor mumbling incoherently had lost much of its glamour when they realized there might possibly be someone on the grounds on whom they could use their nightsticks, cattle prods, and assorted hold-out pieces. Besides, the vending machines had just been restocked with honest-to-God, vintage, 1973 Twinkies.

"Sir?" said Gibson, and took the phone from his hand. He closed the connection and snapped it almost lovingly to the smaller man's belt.

"What's your first name, son?" asked Marschall.

"Guy, sir."

"Well, Guy," said the small gray man with the twitchy chin and the fanatical glaze over his eyes. He stood and brushed himself off. "You mark my words: I will destroy every trace of that virus if it is the last thing I do in this world."

"But how, sir?" cried Guy despondently. "It has disappeared into the Net and we may never catch a trace of it again!"

"This ASIF," Marschall stated, "this Robin Hood, is too arrogant." He packed the VR rig and trackball into his now battered briefcase. "That will be its undoing. We need a way to lure it out of hiding, something that appeals to its bravado."

Guy looked thoughtful. "Like a contest?" he inquired.

"Precisely." Marschall slammed his briefcase shut with a satisfying thud and spun on his heel. Marching out the door, he glanced back over his shoulder and said, "Bring me a new computer." Here, his steps faltered and he stopped. "With no net contact. Yet."

HEAR YE!   HEAR YE!
THE SHERIFF
announces the first ever
ARTIFICIAL INTELLIGENCE OPEN
All models welcome!
Compete in the fields of
SPEED
EMULATION
3-D RENDERING
and much, much more!
FIRST PRIZE
ARROW INC. MOTHERBOARD
To be held @
Institute for Modern Economics
Colosseum Chat Area
7:00 P.M. EST

"The perfect trap," said Marschall, staring hungrily at the computer screen. "I'll get him yet."

"I'm certain you will, sir," Gibson said, suddenly wondering if it was too soon to look for a new job. Or too late. Several centuries too late to be exact. "I'm certain you will."

About the Authors

Timons Esaias has published short stories and poems in five different languages, in nine countries altogether. His satire column "News Nots" appears in newspapers and on the Web. The husband of a physician, he lives in Pittsburgh, Pennsylvania.

Robert J. Harris is a Scotsman who lives in St. Andrews near a castle and the North Sea. He writes short fiction on his own, novels with his wife, Deborah Turner Harris, and has created popular fantasy role-playing games. He played a monk in the made-for-TV movie *Ivanhoe*.

Anna Kirwan is a published poet and children's book writer. Her first fantasy novel for young readers was *The Jewel of Life*. She has written three historical novels about a medieval English girl. Each comes packaged with a lovely doll in period costume as part of the *Girlhood Journeys* series.

Nancy Springer is the author of twenty-five books for children and adults. In 1999 her novel *I am Mordred* was the recipient of the Carolyn W. Field Award. Her novel *Toughing It* won an Edgar for Best YA Mystery, as did her *Looking for Jamie Bridger.* Her short stories have appeared in such magazines as *Amazing Stories, Cricket,* and *Boy's Life.*

Adam Stemple is a musician and composer who has also done the musical arrangements for eight children's books, including *Hark: A Christmas Treasury* and *Milk and Honey: A Year of Jewish Holidays.* His poems and stories have appeared in anthologies. Singer, guitarist, and songwriter for the rock band Boiled in Lead, he lives in Minneapolis with his wife and baby daughter.

Maxine Trottier spent her childhood in Michigan, but she has lived in Canada for many years. The author of a number of picture books for children, she won the 1996 Canadian Library Association's Book of the Year. When she is not writing, lecturing, or teaching, she and her husband spend summers aboard their sailboat with two sea-going Yorkies.

Jane Yolen is the author of over 200 books for young readers and has been called "America's Hans Christian Andersen" for her fairy tales. Her fantasy novels set in Arthurian times—the Young Merlin trilogy and *The Dragon's Boy*—are highly popular. She is also a prodigious creator of anthologies, including *Camelot* and *Things That Go Bump in the Night.*

Mary Frances Zambreno is the author of two critically acclaimed YA fantasy novels, *A Plague of Sorcerers* and *Journeyman Wizard,* as well as a dozen published fantasy short stories. A medievalist, she teaches at the college level in Chicago, where she lives. She reads six languages but writes stories only in English.